Diane,
Friend for 60 years
Never thought we'd be this
Lorraine Valentine x

AT SEA

An Allegory

Lorraine Sharpe

AT SEA

An Allegory

Lorraine Sharpe

Edited by George Meyer

Black Oyster Publishing Company, Inc.

2014

FOR

GEORGE

with whom

I happily travel

Also by the Author

GRACE MAP by Lorraine Valentin Sharpe

DIRTY FEET by Lorraine Valentin Sharpe Meyer

This novel is a work of fiction. Names, characters, places and incidents are either a product of the author's imagination or are used fictitiously.

Copyright @ Casselberry, FL 2015

All rights reserved to the Author

To see the world in a grain of sand

and heaven in a wild flower

Hold infinity in the palm of your hand

and eternity in an hour

Robert Blake

The miracle is not to walk on water.

The miracle is to walk on the green earth

in the present moment.

Thich Nhat Hanh

PROLOGUE

In 1903, Orville Wright and his older brother Wilbur, hooked their bicycle chains from a twelve horsepower gasoline engine to a pair of wooden sticks carved into propellers. They attached their gadget to two sets of homemade wings. Orville climbed aboard the lower wing and took off into the air. He was airborne for twelve seconds, one hundred twenty feet. Flying, controlled by humans rather than wind was born, a giant leap for mankind. Nine years later, the year of Wilbur's death, a plane was flown across the United States in only three months.

On July 15, 1969, only sixty-six years after the Wright brothers' flight, the Apollo eleven spacecraft Columbia launched from Cape Canaveral, Florida for it's first landing on the moon scheduled for July 21st. The whole world had been dreaming, hoping, praying, working to reach the moon.

* * *

Now, seventy-one years after that first launch, flight into outer space, to the moon and to space stations has become available to ordinary travelers.

Binh Renick is one of those travelers, in fact he is preparing for his third voyage and this time he might be given the opportunity for a space-walk. He is as excited embarking on this trip as he had been on his first one.

Not everyone can take advantage of this opportunity, he thought. Lots of guys can't go because their wives are still afraid that something will happen to them out there in space. For some of my friends space flight was a honeymoon venture that they could never afford again once the kids started coming. At forty years of age, I'll probably never find that lucky woman who will call me her "one and only". I might as well enjoy the moon by myself.

Before every space flight, Binh knew, a visit to his grandparents was essential. They had heard the broadcast of the launch of the first flight to the moon from a ship in the Pacific Ocean, the flight that brought Neil Armstrong there for his giant step for mankind. It had been a dramatic moment for his grandparents, one that never seemed to fade in their memories. Now they lived in a condo in Harmony, California overlooking the Pacific Ocean.

Binh, with auburn, wavy hair like his grandfather used to have and ocean blue eyes, had always been the image of his grandfather, Don. It seemed the genes had skipped a generation but came through loud and clear in Binh. His personality was also warm and quiet like his grandfather's. And he dressed as grandma had remembered Don dressing, wearing cozy flannel shirts even with shorts just as Don used to do. Grandma loved having Binh visit. She could almost feel the gentleness of a young Don again when she was in Binh's presence.

"Oh Grandma, isn't it a miracle? I will be flying to the moon again!" Binh said. "When I was a child this was only a dream. Now I'm forty and its a reality. I hope you'll look up and cheer for me during takeoff."

Binh's grandmother, still energetic in her nineties, wearing shorts and a blue tee shirt and sandals with her hair in a loose wedge, had been flitting around the kitchen, making coffee. She walked over and placed a bowl of sliced bananas, peaches and oranges in front of Binh. He got up, took her by the shoulders and sat her down next to him. He winked at her and said, "Grandma, tell me about your experience of the first moon landing."

"Watching the ocean, I never feel too far away from the night of that first flight," she said. "I'm so glad we moved here by the ocean. When I see a space ship land out there in the Pacific it's like reliving those days of the first flight to the moon, when your Grandpa and I were on the ship on the Pacific Ocean. Besides, living here in central California Grandpa and I can see our kids and grandkids often." Grandma got up and went for the coffee pot. "Come on over here Don and sit with Binh while I serve you both" she called to her husband." We don't want to delay him too much."

Binh's grandfather turned from the French window where he spent much of his day. He, like his wife, lived in shorts, tee and sandals. He had a full head of white hair and a mustache. When he wasn't outside working in the garage, he loved watching the ocean and the birds on the beach and the orange and yellow wild flowers. Also in his nineties, Grandpa was still pretty healthy, except for that darn wheelchair that he needed in order to go any distance.

Grandma finished what she was doing and came to sit across from Binh. "Binh I'm so excited for you. When I was young, well, you don't want to hear about ninety years ago right now, but I have so much I want to tell you while I still can," she said. "Most important, remember this:

"The miracle is not that we can fly to the moon or walk on the water or rise from the dead. The miracle is that we walk on this green earth. The miracle is that we receive life by breathing in its air, and give life to others by breathing it out again. The miracle is that the

caterpillar knows how to become a butterfly. The miracle is that human sweat, tears, anger and joy can become a love story that creates and nurtures another human being.

"Binh, always remember that whatever happens in your life, you are that miracle. I want to tell you our story, Grandpa's and mine, to help you understand that, but now may not be the time."

"Oh please, Grandma. I have time. I want to hear your story now."

"Well, okay. You stop me if it gets too long for you. Our story begins on a ship, the California Bear freight ship. That is, it doesn't really begin there. Each of us travelers on that ship had our own stories before we boarded the ship. But it was on the ship that our stories blended and became one. It was a cargo ship which could carry a maximum of twelve passengers. We were eleven who shared one lounge and one dining room for six weeks or more depending on place of disembarking, so we came to know each other quite well. At that time, there was no satellite communication with land from the middle of the ocean. One of the passengers brought a short wave radio, but even that radio had no reception until we were almost to Japan.

"It was 1969, the year of the first moon landing. Our story is the beginning of your story, Binh.

"The first passenger to board the ship was a lady named Beverly. She was from Sweden, a widow who had traveled from her home to the United States to visit her children who lived here. She was returning to the Netherlands on our ship. It took the rest of us a long time to know Beverly because she seemed superficial and needy, but she must have just been lonely, more lonely than she was able to tell us. You'll hear more about her later. Beverly was the self-appointed greeter on our ship that day in 1969. The next person to board was Don. Let me tell you about him."

Chapter 1

DON

Don pulled his new 1969 VW Bug up to the curb in front of his parents' Concord, California wood frame house. It seemed like nothing had changed there since his childhood except the cars, of course. His sisters' cars were already there, Melody's Porsche and Dottie's battered truck. They probably arrived early to help Mom with dinner or to gab, both of which they enjoyed more than Don did. The occasion for this gathering was a going away dinner for Don. Don was always going away, with his work as a free lance writer and photographer, so this party was going a bit too far, but when you received Mom's summons you obeyed or Dad would be hurt. With only three days until embarkation there was so much to do before he left but he couldn't say "no" to Mom.

Don, wearing jeans as usual, his red flannel shirt, matching socks and working boots, jumped out of his yellow bug, stepped back to look it over lovingly. "I'll miss you girl. Be sure that you're looking spanking new and waiting for me when I return. " He planned to leave it here as an extra car for Dad while he was gone not knowing how long he would be away.

After all the hellos the five adults sat down to a scrumptious dinner of his favorite things, prepared just for him even though they didn't go together: salmon, mashed potatoes, Dottie's special baked beans, Melody's asparagus. It was interesting that they all had automatically taken the same places at the dinner table that they had occupied as children. The girls were enthused about his trip and had many questions, Dad was practical like "Be sure you eat enough," and Mom was quiet. When dinner and dishes were finished, Mom took over.

"Donald, sit down." She untied the spotless white apron she always wore when putting dinner on the table. That too hadn't changed since he was eighteen. Also, now as then, Dad had already retired to the front room to escape the clean-up job. Mom instructed Dottie and Melody to follow their father as if she planned a conversation that not even his sisters were allowed to hear.

"You're my only son. You escaped the draft and now you have to volunteer to go over there to Vietnam and get yourself killed." Don couldn't go through this conversation again. When the war started he had already done his tour in the Coast Guard and wasn't drafted. She didn't care why he was not fighting a war only that he wasn't.

"Mom, would you rather have me die young doing something that is important or old and resentful that I had never in my life done anything worthwhile?"

"Don't say things like that. If you stay home and do nothing you're important to us. Your Dad needs you. You're more fun for him than the girls are."

Don couldn't remember ever in his life being described as "fun." He wore a soft shell that hardened like a turtle's in social situations. He had never remembered a good joke no matter how he tried but had ruined many a punch line.

Donald wanted to be somebody. Since he had never been the card, the one who could save the day by making others laugh, he didn't expect that of himself. He just wanted to matter, to know that someone's life was better because of his. He was a bachelor by choice, not afraid of commitment like many other thirty-year-old men. He was very committed to his work. In fact that is why he hadn't married. He was taking risks that a wife or kids did not deserve to have to worry about. Yet he hadn't seen his work as a way of improving those of others. He thought of himself as a useless bystander to the problems he reported on.

His family had always been on his side, his cheerleaders, but didn't always understand him. They were very proud of him when he was published, though Mom thought he should be writing for a respectable paper with job security and a good retirement some day, rather than free-lancing. Mom didn't realize that any good reporter ran a lot of risks. Free-lancing was Don's style. He could take jobs or leave them, could travel or stay home, swim hard or float, live in short term rentals then close up and move. A confirmed bachelor, his sisters said that he just didn't want the limitations demanded by responsible commitment to a family.

Don ended the conversation by getting up from his chair, giving Mom a hug and silently heading for the living room. Over ice cream, Dottie managed to bring laughter back into the room with stories about her pigs giving birth. Even Mom was laughing; not until he was leaving did she again turn weepy.

Don hated himself for leaving Mom in tears but he could see no happy end to this conversation. She would be afraid for him until she saw him again whether he was getting on a ship headed to Vietnam or getting in his bug headed to New York.

"Can we drive you down to the dock?" his dad offered.

"Dad, thanks, but I think that would only start this conversation over and her tears will compete with the volume of the Pacific Ocean.

Let's say "til then" now. I promise to keep in touch whenever I can get a letter out of Vietnam.

And so Don found himself directing a taxi driver around the San Francisco port looking for the gangway of the California Bear. Everything around the dock looked huge but nothing as massive as the Bear when it came in sight. He had only two duffle bags with him for changes during the month before he would alight in Vietnam. Don grabbed the bags, tipped the driver an extra ten because of the mess he would have to extricate himself from around the port, and started up the ramp. He was wearing his best, though worn jeans, sneakers and a plaid flannel shirt. His neat mustache was auburn like his full head of wavy hair. His coloring plus his height at 5'11" would unfortunately be conspicuous among Vietnamese villagers.

Don was boarding the ship two hours early so that he could search out some private escapes before the other travelers arrived, but before he reached the top of the gangway, he heard her voice speaking, apparently to no one.

"Oh good, here comes somebody to talk to. I hate being here alone. Nobody even here to wave me off on the most exciting trip of my life." As Don approached she reached out her right hand to shake his. "Hi, I'm Beverly." Funny how much Beverly reminded Don of Mrs. Slocum of "Are you being Served." In her black and white houndstooth polyester dress and Cuban heels she could have been headed to a senior dance. He would not have been surprised to see her pompadour change from red to blond to even purple during the course of this journey. "Where's the rest of your luggage? Did you preload it?"

"No Ma'am. This is all I'll need."

"Really? Are you getting off early?"

"No Ma'am." How could he escape? "Nice to meet you but I need to see the Captain and check out some things before the others arrive so I'll see you later."

"Oh, I'll help you. I know how to find the Captain. Just come this way." Beverly turned left and started down the port side of the ship. "Your name is?"

"I'm Don." Don didn't really want to meet the Captain but why not let Beverly do her good deed and get this over with. He figured she'd direct him and then leave him. "Okay Beverly, lead on to the Captain."

Beverly seemed to know her way around the ship already and didn't hesitate to knock on Captain Engle's door. "Captain, its me, Beverly. I know I shouldn't be in your quarters right now but a gentleman passenger here wants to see you and I'm just helping him."

"Just a few minutes." The captain's hesitant response had a yawn built in. He was probably catching his last snooze before launch.

"Thank you Beverly. I'll take care of myself now." Don said, feeling awkward barging in on the captain early, but Beverly didn't feel embarrassed at all. "I'll let you have some privacy. Let me know if you need anything else." Off she waltzed to await the next passenger to board.

A minute later Captain Mack Engle peaked out his cracked doorway. He was wearing a white tee with sleeves rolled, jeans and bare feet. His straight grey hair brushed the top of his black rimmed glasses. "Do you need help now? I'll be on deck when it's time for everyone to board but this is a little early."

Don was apologetic. "No Captain, I don't need you now. I kind of got trapped into following Beverly. She was only trying to help."

Captain Engle rolled his eyes. "Good, I'll see you later. We'll have lots of time during the next few weeks. If you see Beverly, … never mind." He closed the door and Don could hear him pull the chain.

Not many people traveled by freighter anymore. As a matter of fact, the Bear Line observed the no more than twelve passengers rule. If the ship carried one more, even a baby, law required a medical staff on board. No one seemed to worry about one of the twelve needing medical care. Or how about the sixty crew? Guess they could just be thrown overboard or walk the plank if an accident or act of God or man left them fatally wounded.

Don was sure a freighter was the right choice for this trip. It wasn't any cheaper than flying, but the price included all meals and room for the twenty-two days it would take to cross the Pacific and more days to arrive at his point of disembarking. He could use the ship as a hotel and restaurant while it was docked in each port for unloading. Since cargo was priority for freight ships the ship could be dock side for many days if the weather did not allow opening the hold for loading and unloading. That gave plenty of time for passengers to tour the port cities.

The California Bear was scheduled to dock at Yokohama and Kobe Japan; Pusan, Korea; Okinawa; Taipei, Taiwan; Manila, Philippines; Bangkok, Thailand and Haiphong, South Vietnam where Don would be alighting, before it headed to the Netherlands across the Atlantic and finally around Cape Horn and all the way back to San Francisco.

Don wanted lots of time to think. With only eleven fellow travelers instead of thousands and no scheduled entertainment like on cruise ships, surely he'd have lots of time to be alone. Vietnam was in the middle of war and his country, some thought, was the bad guy. How would the Vietnamese people tolerate or treat him?

In 1967 Don had gone to Vietnam as an on sight photographer for the National Catholic Reporter and to interview the man on the street in Haiphong. Don was devastated by the tragedy and inspired by the gentleness of the people he interviewed. His feelings were so intense and so jumbled. He felt defeat and helplessness in the face of their disaster. But he felt such admiration for how they were handling it, helping each other at great cost to themselves, sometimes even helping friendly or enemy soldiers.

When in Haiphong Don had met Harlan Conway. Harlan, a small man with the determination of Napoleon and the kindness of Jesus, had come to Vietnam with an independent "Rescue the Refugee" group which had disbanded in disillusionment after a short stay. But Harlan had become attached to some of the parentless, homeless kids and chose to stay and do what he could. Sometimes he slept on the street with the kids but most of the time he managed to drag kids that he connected with, to one of the various shelters established by religious or civic groups.

Don returned home and published his story as he had planned. After the article was published Don would sit and look at the photos it carried, remembering five year old Binh carrying his baby sister Cara, to the garbage pit to look for food and Harlan carrying little Bay away from the dead body of her big sister. Telling their story wasn't fixing their story. He had to find a way to help and not just write about what he saw. Maybe if he lived among them he'd know how they felt, how their parents must feel when they couldn't save their children. Maybe if he could fix the feeling for just one of them he'd know that his own life mattered. He couldn't wait any longer. He wrote to Harlan via a military site he had been referred to and was amazed when he received a response just a month later.

Harlan had been hoping to establish a hostel for the kids and maybe with Don's help he would be able to do so. He welcomed Don to join him in his work but he warned him that if he did so he could return home minus a limb or two or not at all. Don was already thirty.

If he didn't do something worthwhile with his life now, would he ever? That same day Don made a reservation for travel on the California Bear leaving in June for Asia. Don would disembark in Haiphong where Harlan hoped to be able to meet Him.

After leaving Captain Engle, Don took the iron steps to the fourth deck where the sign clearly read "passengers." Strolling down the starboard side he noticed the entrance to an open room marked "lounge." The lounge was about twenty feet by twenty feet square. The floor was covered with brown indoor/outdoor type carpeting. In the lounge was one card table with six metal chairs, four single cushioned lounging chairs and one two-seat sofa. Each stuffed chair had a magazine rack at its side and unmatching lamps, probably obtained from local garage sales. He turned on the switch which lit a center plain, rather dim chandelier. There was no odor at all. The room was clean. In one corner was an easel and a stack of canvases and black plastic bag, someone's junk. What could anyone paint here? It looked like a place where people would be bored. He'd surely be anxious to get off this ship after a month in this suite.

Two doorways on each of three sides of the room stood open exposing pairs of single beds. The fourth wall had only windows to the starboard deck and ocean view. Don circled the room and found name plates identifying passengers' space at each cabin door. There he found his name, his name only, Donald Renick at one of the doors. How had he been so lucky to have his own private room?

He moseyed around the lounge checking the names at the other doors, two names each, returned to his room, dropped his duffle bags, plopped down and stretched out on his bed. He looked at the ceiling. That was fine, no water marks, no leaks. The closet would hold everything he brought. The simplicity of the quarters suited him but it was dawning on him that he would be living awfully close to the likes of Beverly and the other ten for the next few weeks. Don jumped up and looked out his porthole to the port side of the ship. The ship was being loaded with noisy equipment by noisier men.

The port-side door to the deck was locked so Don returned to the door he had entered. There seemed to be no one around to ask, so he walked around the ship to the port side in time to watch a string of eight garbage trucks being hoisted up and into the hold. They fit easily in the hold like eight chihuahuas on a football field. He could have watched, amazed, for hours but he was on a mission to locate his getaways, so he continued around the deck to the next upward bound iron steps. He finally came to the top on level eight. A couple of sections about ten feet square were railed off. Benches were positioned to look forward and aft and nailed down. This might be a perfect place to be alone. How often would people like Beverly climb four flights of iron steps, one and a half stories each, to sit up here and look at more ocean?

Don sat on one of the forward looking benches thinking about the journey that would take him under the Golden Gate Bridge to the bombed out muddy streets of Vietnam. Would Harlan be there to meet him as he hoped? Would he too, like Harlan, be sleeping on the street? What would that be like? Cold? Wet? Scary people waiting for a chance to rob you? Was he only depriving the kids of needed food by taking some of it for himself? Would he be able to get back if he changed his mind? Why, really, was he doing this?

Despite the fears that kept impinging on his thoughts Don was sure of his decision. He had no family of his own that was dependent on his safety, yet his life would matter to someone, to the kids. He had always envied people who knew how to make others laugh, those whose names everyone knew. Now he experienced an awareness that he was headed for the life he was made for. He would be important to people that no one else cared about and even they wouldn't know how important he was to them. His optimism felt warm and snug, then became a doze in the California sun on the California Bear.

Meanwhile Beverly was busily supervising the on-ramp and the few arriving passengers, and imagining that Don and Captain Mack were in the Captain's quarters toasting the impending voyage.

* * *

Grandpa interrupted. "That Beverly was something, but I want to tell about the brother and sister, Debra and Barry Andover who boarded the ship together. They seemed to care so much for each other. "They were inseparable at first. Barry had one purpose, rescuing Debra." Debra was trying desperately to rescue herself. She was our real success story."

* * *

Chapter 2

DEBRA and BARRY

"Debra, I cannot think of any other way to help you. For the second time, you've checked yourself out of the rehab I've been paying for. You're thin as a stick. You're not eating. You're on the street when I don't support you. You crash at my place whenever you hit rock bottom and decide to get help. Then, just when you're starting to show signs of life, you disappear on me until you become desperate again." He took a breath. Talking to her was useless, but he couldn't stop.

"I have a job at a bank. Maybe I don't like being in an office counting money all day but it pays my way and it pays for the nice place where you crash on a whim. If my boss knew I was supporting here every day. With this application she could at least show Barry that she had started to search. That would buy her time in his condo.

Debra exhaled a sigh of relief after completing the application the best that she could, and wandered aimlessly out of Wendy's. How could she hang on the streets and stay clean? So far she had managed for two weeks since walking from that military rule, stifling rehab center. As she sauntered along she noticed a cluster of pale pink flowering plum trees surrounding a splashing pond. How unusual right here on a residential city street. Next to the pond was a sign reading,

WELCOME

Open to Everyone, Please enter

Meditation Thursdays at 7 P.M.

Lessons on Request

More curious about the beautiful fragrant plum trees and gushing pond than about the invitation to meditation, Debra turned onto the brick pavered walk. She hesitated when she saw the bald headed, orange robed man at the far end of the winding walk, but he noticed her and beckoned her forward. He didn't seem to mean she should approach, only that it was okay to enter. What a cool place, so quiet that the birds had a voice. As she neared the monk she felt the need to apologize to him, "I'm not here for lessons or anything. I only thought it looked like a beautiful walk."

"It is a beautiful walk. It is a place of beauty, peace and joy. Come as often as you like," he encouraged. "My name is Nai Saum. Please ask for me at the office if you need help at any time."

Debra felt tears almost choke her as they suddenly ran down her throat. She hadn't realized how relieved she would feel after being unburdened of the desperate need for daily drugs. Maybe she was on her way after all, clean for six weeks now. She felt her shoulders suddenly relax. It felt like the wrinkles on her face smoothed out. Maybe life could be better than it had been lately. She could hardly wait to tell Barry about her day. Surely he'd let her stay with him awhile now.

When she returned to the condo, she got the phone call she had dreaded. She was accepted for the job at Wendy's and could start next week. The manager said she needed to stop by and pick up her medical screening forms and get to the clinic for approval before next Monday. Suddenly and unexpectedly, Debra was employed. Would the needle marks on her arms be a problem in the clinic? She knew she should no longer have drugs in her system, but the needle marks? Maybe the doctor wouldn't notice them if she wore long sleeves. What about the nurse taking her blood pressure?

Besides the medical exam, she was frightened of the workplace the daily routine and responsibility, but knew she could do it, she had to do it. Maybe she could get some control of her life again. She could pay Barry a little, eat at work, spend time in the Buddhist Gardens and save a little money until she could get a better job and move out to her own place. She'd ask Barry to keep her money so that she couldn't use it on drugs when times got tougher.

Barry sounded very pleased with the news she blasted at him when he opened the door. It meant putting up with her longer, he realized, and helping her through her struggle. He had no doubt it would be hard. The pain of it all wouldn't be over this easily. All day he had worried about whether he had done the right thing by threatening her this morning. Now he knew that he had. She might not succeed, but she'd started on her way.

Barry hurried to change clothes. Debra was hoping he would go with her to pick up her forms. As soon as he was ready, they headed to Wendy's so she could accept the job in person and pick up the medical screening forms.

"Let's have dinner here so you can picture yourself waiting on us," Barry suggested.

They got in the regular line with seven customers ahead of them. After standing there a minute and observing the people ahead of them Debra said, "First thing I'd change if I could, would be to put signs down lower so these old people with bifocals could read them. That would make the line move faster and help the customers, too."

There's a little bit of the old Debra, Barry thought. She's already going to fix this place before she even starts work. I'm so happy to see her like this, I could dance.

That night as Debra was falling asleep she kept hearing Nai Saum's words, "a place of beauty, peace and joy." Could she do it? Stay off the coke, not even a fag, and still find peace and joy? She'd try, one day at a time as she was taught. It had been a long time since she'd had a good night's sleep without chemical help. Tonight she would sleep...finally, and she did.

When Debra went to the clinic for her check-up she was scared and sweating. The nurse pulled up her sleeves to take her blood pressure and asked, "Debra, are you on drugs?" Well, here goes the job, Debra thought, but she had decided not to lie. It would only be worse if they found out later.

"I used to be," she said, but I've been clean since I was in Rehab." She avoided saying how long that had been. The doctor didn't ask again and it wasn't until she was handed a pink slip on the way out of the office, that Debra knew if she would be approved or not. The Wendy's form was stamped "Approved for work". "Just bring this in to your new employer," she was told by the check out clerk as she left the clinic.

The job started out with a week of orientation. By the end of the week Debra felt confident and hopeful. Although edgy, she was too busy to think about missing a fix most of the time. It was the downtime that was really hard, when the ghost struck. In a panic she would ask other employees to take a break and let her cover for them to keep busy. Maybe if she asked Nai Saum about lessons she could help herself get past the craving and get through the down times a little easier.

Barry thought the meditation lessons were a little overkill but Debra talked him into at least walking in the gardens with her, so that he'd understand better, the experience she was having there. He had to admit he enjoyed the peace and quiet and within a few weeks he was stopping there for thirty minutes every day on the way home from work.

One day at the monastery Debra asked Nai Saum what she should do to become Buddhist.

"Don't think about becoming Buddhist," Nai Saum said. "Just learn to practice, to meditate and Buddha will guide your understanding. Then you will know if being a Buddhist is the best way for you to learn to be compassionate and peaceful."

"Where should I go to learn this? she asked."

"Go inside yourself, he said simply."

Debra was terrified. She was afraid to tell the monk about her drug problem for fear he would not want her to come there any more. She felt stretched like a tight rope. She was having night sweats and shakes. She had so far, resisted several opportunities to get just a small quick fix. If she fell, she was convinced, she'd never be strong enough to climb back out of the hole. But "go inside yourself?" There was nothing inside herself to go to. Go inside yourself wouldn't work for her.

Then she remembered her imaginings the day she saw in passing, that freight ship ad. It couldn't hurt to check it out, and so the journey began. She was re-routed, and hung-up-on, and put on hold many times during her beginning search but she had an idea she wouldn't let die. Finally she had enough information about traveling by freight ships, to explain her idea to Barry. She still had no idea what would happen when she got to the Orient.

"I've been hoping that my money, that you're saving for me, would eventually be a down payment on an apartment so I could get out of your hair, Barry, but there is something else I want to do. I'll need all of my money and some of your help besides." As Debra explained the venture to Barry, she became more sure of herself and more determined to make it work. "It would take me almost a month on the ship or maybe more, to get to the Orient. I wouldn't have any access to drugs and maybe I would get a little more past my craving. Then I'll get off the ship in Japan or Thailand where I won't need too much money."

"Deb, don't you know that those countries are full of drugs? You'll be lonely and not have any support to help you say 'no'".

"I'll go to a Buddhist temple and ask the monks to teach me about Buddhism. Maybe I can find that peace they're talking about."

"You're so unrealistic. What makes you think you can heal better in a foreign land? How do you know the monks would admit you?"

During the next month Debra never hesitated in her pursuit or in her coaxing of Barry. Although Barry never caught her enthusiasm about Buddhism his interest and conversation gradually changed. First it was, "a freight ship? That's crazy," then "A freight ship would be a great experience. I've never done anything crazy like that before." Then it was   "If I go, I would prefer Japan because I might find work there and be able to keep you off the street."

Finally Barry said "yes," arranged for a leave of absence from work, and with Debra, set a departure date and made a reservation on the California Bear. They would share a room and be in Kobe, Japan by the end of the summer.

* * *

Grandma had gotten up to warm their coffee, then she went on with the story. "Then there was our peacemaker, Lillian Small. What a great woman she was. She was a pianist and an artist. She often busied herself with sketching, but our small quarters didn't lend themselves to much art, except of course sunrises and sunsets and portraits of all of us. And she enjoyed doing portraits. How I wish I had the portraits she did of each of us. But mainly she wanted to paint the ports and all the activity in the ports."

* * *

Chapter 3

LILLIAN

When Jerry called Lillian to invite her to dinner on the last evening before her trip, she was ambivalent. She couldn't say no to the best friend a girl ever had. Maybe she had filled her schedule that week to avoid having to face the moment of goodbyes. Jerry loved her and wanted to marry her. Lillian had decided to take a ship around the world by herself.

"Jerry, if I marry anyone it will be you, but right at this moment I want to be on my own. I'm loving my freedom."

It was only a week since Lillian had given the last piano lesson. She had been teaching piano all of her life it seemed. Even before she met Joe, Lillian supported herself by teaching piano. She had students of all ages, and helped a few of them who were motivated, establish their own careers in music. When her kids were young it was a perfect profession for her as she could establish her own hours and be there for them when they came home from school. When Joe was so sick from heart failure, she was able to be with him, lighten her teaching schedule and return to a fuller schedule after he died. At seventy years of age it was time to give up work, even a work she loved, and do something adventurous.

"I married at eighteen, raised three kids and more dogs and rabbits and lizards. I've cared for a sick husband and worked until last week. I've loved all of it until now but now the thought of being restricted again makes me want to explode. Can you understand that?"

"I'll try to understand and I'll promise not to restrict you."

"But Jerry, I'll restrict me. I'll always tell myself I have to think of you. I want to be wild til I'm tired of it. Then if I'm not dead, we'll see. If I married you now I'd always be hoping that you'd die soon so I could have my chance to sprout wings and fly before I'm too old." Lillian was amused at herself, pleased that she was able to be this honest with Jerry. Jerry's long face notwithstanding, she continued,

"Tomorrow night I have to save for the surprise party the kids are having for me. You can take me to the ship for preloading my stuff if you want. Then come to my party and we'll say 'toodle ooo' til 1970. You know I love you but I really want you to see me off this way. Its too hard for me to say a romantic 'goodbye.'" Lillian flipped her new wedge doo and took Jerry's hand. She kissed his lips lightheartedly. He put his arm around her waist, then patted her great little butt. Seemed like that was about all he was gonna get for now.

"I'll be at your place early tomorrow so we can have lunch before going to the dock. I'll pick the restaurant because it has to be special and you would have us eating at McDonalds," he said.

The next day Jerry was at Lillian's house at 11:00 to take her to their favorite Italian hideout, chosen because it was kept dark enough for candlelight even at lunch time. They sat on the same side of the booth and shared a bottle of Chianti during a lazy lunch, then headed to the dock in Jerry's Jag with the lid down.

Pre-loading was a project for Lillian. She had art supplies: paints, brushes, chalk, pens, ink, canvases, sketch pads, enough stuff to reproduce all the ports around the world. None of her things could be stashed below. She would need her supplies for the journey. Besides her own shoes, dresses, night clothes she carried gifts for all the kids in every port, not just candy and soap, but harmonicas, little flutes and keyboards and drums, kazoos made from combs covered with wax paper and bound by rubber bands. She planned to teach the joy of music to the little urchins every chance she got. Hopefully the other passengers would tolerate her use of a little extra space for her stuff.

Lillian's surprise party at her son Larry's house went off as she had planned it. Her daughter and two sons, their spouses and seven grandchildren were all surprised at how surprised she managed to be. Although her children had reservations about the wisdom of her trip they put all those aside for tonight to spend the evening making merry. The children's rendition of "Gramma row your boat ashore, Alleluia" and

"Row, row, row your boat Grandma down the stream

Merrily merrily merrily merrily life is but a dream"

closed off the evening with laughter and happy tears wetting everyone's cheeks.

Her kids wouldn't hear of any other send-off the next day, than having all their kids excused from school so they could come en-mass to the ship. When they arrived at the dock they had to park and walk two blocks with the children in hand, but when they got to the ship the excited seven children from Mickie, age ten carrying her sister of six months down to two year old Ryan raced up the ramp first and landed in the arms of Beverly. The last person on board was Lillian.

"Are all these lovely children going with us?" Beverly asked, knowing it couldn't be. "Oh I'm so happy to meet my cabin mate," she exclaimed when Lillian introduced herself. The two women could not have been more different, Lillian's brown and white tweed wedge was blowing loosely, her tight navy slacks, white socks, white shirt with a sailor collar, her gift from the kids, and red cardigan sweater somehow looked classy on her thin shapely five-foot two figure.

"I'm here for the ride," Lillian told her excitedly, "going all the way around."

"I get off in the Netherlands," Beverly responded, "So you'll have some peace and quiet the last half of your trip."

In Lillian's room her daughter expressed her concern, "Mom, if you and Beverly don't like each other maybe you can ask for a room change. Beverly is so, well different."

"Joan, different is what I want. By the time we get off this ship I'll be wearing cuban heels and Beverly will be doing cartwheels. We are going to be a hilarious pair. Life has never been better. Now Joan, take the children off this ship so they have time to see all the exciting things around the port before dark. And Jerry, get him off too. How many times and ways can one say 'I love you and I'm waiting for you.' It will be much more fun looking five stories down at him and waving from here."

So, like a shepherd who found a really big lost sheep, Joan put her arms around Jerry's waist and dragged him toward the downward ramp behind all the children with their dads. In big "sigh" language Lillian paraphrased "Free at last, free at last, Thank God Almighty I'm free at last."

* * *

"Daiki was our only Asian on board, even though we were to make many stops in Asian countries. He had grown up being always proper and a little stoic. Well, that couldn't last too long among us," laughed Grandpa. "I've always wondered how he made out after he disembarked. For all we know, he could be in California. Binh, when you get back, maybe you could help us with a computer search for Daiki, and maybe Debra Kajikawa. Well here is his story as far as we know it."

* * *

Chapter Four

DAIKI

Japan to San Francisco had not been as difficult as Daiki had expected. He had already crossed the language bridge and spoke English easily. The two cities were similar at least down by the wharf near his San Francisco digs, too many people, too much noise, constant commotion. As an observer, he loved it all. He missed his family and friends though. He had never had time for play, growing up in Japan. He had spent his whole childhood studying and competing in school. It paid off when he was one of only three students accepted into an exchange program and sent to complete a master's degree in journalism at Berkeley University. His internship at the San Francisco Chronicle continued his preparation.

San Francisco back to Yokohama, Japan though, might not be as simple. Can one ever go home? Now he would have to support himself. Workplace competition might not come as naturally to him as academic competition had. The slow boat to Yokohama would give Daiki time to be mentally ready for work. Now he knew why some American commuters find, that an hour on the freeway, prepares their mind for work on the morning after whatever-they were-up-to the night before. They actually like that freeway ride.

Daiki was tall for a Japanese man of his era. At six feet, he would stand out in any Japanese setting even more than he had in America. Apart from a little track and hiking the San Francisco hills, he had not been active in sports. Besides that, he had kept pretty much on a Japanese diet, and so maintained his slim build and trim appearance. He arrived at the ship wearing black, tailored slacks, shiny black leather shoes and a white pressed short sleeve shirt. He carried one large suitcase and an overstuffed leather briefcase. He planned to keep daily notes about his voyage in preparation for a future article. More importantly during free time in San Francisco, he had made many phone calls and done library research as a head start to his job search. He would have time to design a resume' appropriate for each individual position for which he hoped to interview.

Now the day was here. He was returning to his family including five younger siblings, mom and dad, three grandparents and an aunt and uncle all in a five room house, and to his school friends. He was a different person than when he left them five years ago. Now he was educated for his life's work, knowledgeable, experienced and not so obviously, terrified. He wondered if he was good enough to compete and make an independent living in the competitive Japanese media.

As for all the other passengers, Beverly was waiting for Daiki when he reached the top of the gangway. "Wow!" She looked way up into his brown eyes and continued to the top of his head, then back down all the way. Why wasn't I born twenty-five years later?"

Daiki blushed with surprise, too perplexed to respond. He could never get used to Americans being so outspoken. He pretended he hadn't heard and continued to follow the gentleman who had boarded just ahead of him up the iron steps to the fourth level of the ship. They both hesitated as they reached the lounge, noted other passengers milling around there and noticed name plates at each door. They both crossed the lounge, checked the names at the doorways, stopped at the same door, turned to look at each other, point to each other and laugh."

"You're my pair," the other man said. They dropped their bags and reached out their right hands to shake. "I'm Goose," the "pair" said.

"Hi, I'm Daiki Kajikawa, Goose? Daiki look quizzically at the other name plate by his door that read John Ash, not Goose.

"Oh that? Just call me Goose."

"Okay, Goose."

They picked up their bags and entered the room. It was hard for Daiki to tell Goose's age. He stood erect, wore jeans, his biceps bulging from the blue tee like yeasted dough from too small a bread pan, his skin was dark tan and leathery. His fingers were yellowed like a long time smoker but there was no tobacco odor on his breath or clothes and his teeth were white and perfect, maybe false. Even a Japanese like Daiki could recognize Tennessee when he spoke.

"Hain't no sense in hankerin' over what bed to lie in Daiki. I ain't got no trouble holdin' it in at night sos I don't need to be by the head," Goose said as he dropped his bags by the left side bed furthest from the bathroom. Goose looked out his porthole. "I'm aimin' to pace the deck 'til tootin' time so you take your time settin' in if you want."

As Goose turned to leave the room Daiki smiling, cocked his head like a poodle does, when it's straining so hard to know the meaning of the words it's hearing. He shook his head a little. I've just met my first on-ship story he thought as he began settin' in. He couldn't wait to hear more about Goose. This trip would be fun.

* * *

"I have to be the one to tell you Liesl's story, Binh, Grandpa said. Pay close attention to Liesl's story, I know you'll never forget it."

* * *

Chapter 5

LIESL

Liesl Victorine and her partner Sister Ethel McMahon, Sisters of the religious order of St. Victor, planned to travel to Thailand by freight ship. The purpose of their trip was to establish a clinic in a small town which had a large percentage of residents with Hansen's Disease and no medical facility. She and her partner had experience obtained at the United States Public Health Service Hospital in Louisiana. Sister Ethel would be the Superior of this enterprise, in charge of the work and in charge of Liesl.

Sister Ethel had entered the religious community at age thirty-five and was now sixty. Liesl felt sure that Sister Ethel, having seen a lot of the world as a lay person, would be more mature, more experienced, and consequently more laid back about community rules than the Superiors that she had previously experienced. Maybe this exciting adventure would fulfill the dream she had as a teen.

When Liesl was seventeen she could probably have had many or any boyfriend she wanted. At five foot six inches tall and slender, with brown almost black wavy hair, her big brown eyes said "welcome" to everyone she met. But being flat chested and tomboyish she didn't think of herself as sexy or even attractive. Like many of her friends, she began her working career at age sixteen, accepting a nurses' aide position at Los Angeles County Hospital. Liesl was assigned to a large ward to which nursing home residents or street people were usually admitted. On her first morning she arrived for the 7:00 A.M. morning report as she had been told to do.

"Liesl, the man in room 222 just died and the night staff didn't have time to clean up his body. Will you please do that while we're listening to report? The supplies are in his room," Mrs. Fredricks her head nurse directed.

It was her first experience with a dead body. Liesl trying not to let her hesitance show turned quickly and headed down to room 222. She found towels, washcloths, a canvas body bag and a cardboard tag with a place for name, date and time and a wire string for tying onto his toe. Though some teens would have been dumbfounded by this experience, Liesl swallowed deep, blinked hard and did the job, feeling very proud that she had been trusted with such an important job her first morning. Later that day Liesl stopped in the ward to check on a blind patient to whom she had been assigned.

"Mrs. Grant, its me, Liesl. I'm just going to take your temperature and pulse if its okay. Your nurse asked me to look at your dressing to see if its dry. May I lift your covers to look at it please?"

"Of course you may, Liesl. Thank you."

The next morning at change of shift report Mrs. Fredricks used the time when the staff was all gathered, as she often did, for a brief encouraging or educational moment. "Yesterday I noticed Liesl taking care of Mrs. Grant. When she entered the room and before touching her, she told Mrs. Grant who she was and what she planned to do. Imagine being blind and lying in that bed. Would you not be afraid whenever someone entered if you didn't know what they were going to do to you next? Good job Liesl."

Leisl didn't realize she had done anything good or unusual. She just knew how scary it must be to be touched unexpectedly when you're feeling so helpless, lying in a bed with side rails and unable to see. She was so happy she had done well. Caring for people like Mrs. Grant must come natural to her.

Liesl worked hard all summer and the next year after school. She often had funny stories to take home, like the time ninety-year-old Bridget used her water pitcher for a urinal and Mrs. Fredrick almost tasted it to see what it was. And the time she left a red haired patient to fill her water pitcher and returned to find without warning, that the patient was bald. When a patient was difficult for her, Liesl would stop outside the door before entering and remind herself, "I am taking God's place, caring for this patient. I'll take care of her the way He would."

At seventeen years of age Liesl felt unsettled. Her high school days were about to end and she knew she was making a choice that would drive the rest of her life. She followed suggestions made by experts on decision making: establish an equation, not pros in the left column and cons in the right but pros of one choice on the left and pros of the other choice on the right. Each time she started with the pros on the left, whatever item was first on her list took on such power that it would send her on a tangent and she could not complete her list.

Left column first, children. She pictured her own children sitting on a big bed at story time as she had done beside her brothers Collen and Keith. They would be blond like her prince and brown-eyed like herself. They would snuggle close to her in their flannel pajamas, giggle and pick on their toes as she read bedside stories to them. When she tried again her list was topped by Prince Charming taking her hand as they walked laughing, in the woods. Her left column was long but to her, felt unrewarding. That list always ended with herself shopping, cooking, drinking coffee, happy in an inconsequential world. Always it made her feel bound to her roots, bound was the important word. Liesl who felt urged to go, to search, to find, on this list only felt bound.

Then she tried the right column. Here she could not make much of a list, it all came down to one thing. On the right Liesl wrote, "I may be lonely and my future unknown, but I will be free to climb, to search, to be stretched, to give my all. There will be no family expectations, no one I have to imitate or match (and conversely no one to praise or love me.) I will be in search of my dream. As a nun I will belong only to God and, if He chooses, I will also belong to the poor.

Liesl took her lists and walked out onto the tree shaded porch. She sat in the rocker that was in a patch of sun. Out beneath the tree, polka dots of sun were dancing. She didn't need to look over her lists. No matter how painful it would be to leave her beloved home and family she almost had no choice. She knew, as seventeen year olds know, that she could never give herself to anyone with the intensity with which she could give herself to God. If she stayed rooted at home or with her own family, she would always wish she had been braver.

The thought of starting out on this climb, of abandoning herself to an unknown path, unattached, made her ecstatic. The dancing polka dots seemed so much more exciting than the patch of sun that never moved.

Some people know they want to be a veterinarian because they love animals or a nurse because they had a good hospital experience or a concert pianist because they're good at it. Not Liesl She wanted to belong to God. It didn't matter to her what profession or occupation she practiced. She figured from reading Jesus' story that taking care of those who were poor was the way to belong to God. You could do this teaching, nursing or in so many other occupations. She would be a nun. Then she could be poor herself and be assured that her life would be filled with opportunities to help others poor like herself.

As soon as she was accepted she entered the St. Victor Community of Sisters. Her first years were horrible for her but she was determined to stick it out. Every Sunday afternoon at letter-writing time, Liesl spent in tears, she was so homesick. Her letters home always sounded upbeat. She could do it. She kept her goal in mind and bravely completed two years of novitiate, then four more years of nursing education. Although she felt stifled by community rules, she told herself that this was necessary during times of training. She would feel free once she began the work she was aching to do. Finally and happily she accepted her first assignment to Columbia Hospital in Nashville, Tennessee.

Then reality struck again. The poor, where were they? She had chosen this community because it was noted for service to the poor. None of the other sisters seemed concerned that they were living in an ivory tower with great food and sterile quarters and spending their time doing administrative work. There were so many simple people from the hill country around Nashville who became patients. Their family members took two or three buses to come to visit and seemed very tired when they arrived. After an hour sitting in a straight metal chair at the bedside of their loved one in the ward, they would have to begin the trek home often to waiting, hungry children or to their elderly spouse. Then Liesl was expected to leave the ward sit down with the other sisters and enjoy a big bowl of ice cream in complete comfort and no worries.

"Since you have been assigned to learn hospital administration you shouldn't feel guilty about being coddled, as you call it. You should accept this as God's will for you," she was told when she expressed her discontent to her supervisor. Liesl alone found opportunities to drive into the hills to visit patients that she knew needed help. But her peer sisters looked askance at her, judging that she was attempting to be different than or better than them.

Her frustration became a crisis for her one evening. Mrs. Stephan, the wife of Fred Stephan who had major surgery planned to stay with him the night before his discharge from the hospital. The loud speaker system announced the end of visiting hours at 8:30 P.M. At 9:00 Liesl hesitatingly, reminded Mrs. Stephan that it was time to leave the hospital. Mrs. Stephan refused, saying she planned to sit in the chair for the night and would not bother Fred or his roommate. When Liesl, having accepted this variance, returned to the station her mentor stopped her.

"Liesl, you are learning supervision and you must learn to be firm and authoritative in this job."

Feeling torn and bewildered, Liesl returned as she was directed to do, to Mrs. Stephan and insisted that she leave. When his wife had gone, Fred went into the bathroom to get ready to turn in for the night. After twenty minutes, his roommate called his nurse to say he had never come out of the bathroom. The nurse found him dead on the bathroom floor. It was Liesl's job to call his wife and ask her to return to the hospital. Then she had to meet her when she returned with the news of his death.

Liesl was awake all night enraged at herself for obeying an unreasonable demand. After this devastating experience immediately the next morning, she told her community manager that she must have a change in assignments. She could not be in a position to enforce rules she did not believe in. She knew she was not cut out for making and imposing rules on other people. Who said God's will for her was God's will for them too? She had realized the night before that she was too inexperienced to know when she should fight the system and when obey it.

At her request Liesl was next assigned to a staff nurse position in a hospital specializing in care of people with Hansen's Disease. This work was much more suited to her but she continued to feel restricted, too separated from the people that she was learning to love. She felt belittled by her peers. Every effort to genuinely connect with a patient was met by them with suspicion.

Since her current situation was the only one in the United States in which the sisters did staff nursing, Liesl requested a missionary assignment in an underdeveloped country where she thought there would be less scrutiny and she would be more free to serve people in need. She was now thirty years old, still always searching, always wanting to be among "the least of these" in a personal serving capacity, not in an administrative one. When would she find the life that she had been longing for all these years?

"I'd rather die from smoking cigarettes than from second hand smoke," she told her superiors in an effort to explain her negative feelings about administrative jobs. "I want to work with people, not be protected from them." Yet she felt certain that, as she had been called to a religious community by God. There had to be a way to make this work for her.

She therefore accepted assignment to a new mission in northeast Thailand. Liesl and Ethel, manager of the enterprise and her religious superior, would live in a small town in northeast Thailand which had at one time been a hideaway for people with Leprosy and so continued to have a large percentage of residents with this disease. Their job would be to establish a clinic and to teach local nurses how to diagnose, treat and care for these residents as well as for the general population.

Liesl and Ethel, met in San Francisco the morning of their departure. After an adventurous afternoon at the San Francisco port and dinner with two former Hansen's Disease patients who had welcomed them to the city, they boarded the California Bear at 5:30 P.M. They were both dressed in their white "habits," the uniform dress of their religious community. Liesl carried her guitar in a beautiful case that her two brothers and their families had given her as a going away gift. She also carried music and Thai language study materials to occupy her time on the ship. Sister Ethel carried a satchel full of games, cards and treats that she thought might be needed by all the travelers en route. When Beverly saw the two nuns boarding she rolled her eyes and said to Debra who happened to walk by,

"Well, it looks like we'll have to toe the mark on this boat."

"Maybe it will be good for us, Beverly."

"Don't say that Debra. You'll bring us bad luck." To the Sisters she said, "Good Afternoon. Will you be traveling with us? I promise to be good, Ha ha, if I can stand to for so long."

Debra interrupted Beverly's attempt at humor. Beverly was obviously uncomfortable with the Sisters. Debra felt she was expressing her anxiety with total rudeness and tried to help.

"Hi, I'm Debra. Looks like we'll have some music on board. I look forward to talking with you later, she said to Liesl. " I play a little guitar too, but I don't have one with me. Maybe we can lead some music together." Liesl smiled at her, and nodded gratefully but kept walking, while Ethel stopped. She was busy being cordial. Liesl reached the lounge, found their nameplates by their cabin door and lay her guitar and bags on the bed to the left. She looked out the porthole which faced the starboard side of the boat. She was overwhelmed by ambivalent feelings. She was so excited to be traveling to Thailand by ship after having lead such a quiet life. The wonder of it all felt strange though. She had always loved leading a simple life. Yet she was so happy to be doing something exciting for a change. Did this mean it was the time in her life to start taking initiative, to make the changes she sought, rather than demanding herself to obey other people's rules? Maybe she really needed more excitement.

She absentmindedly watched the boat being loaded. Although an artist at heart, she barely noticed the waves around the dock reflecting the blue sky. Her thoughts were elsewhere. It made her uncomfortable to realize that the people with whom she would live for the next month had no idea of what kind of "animal" a nun was. Liesl didn't even know herself if the word "nun" described her. The anticipated freedom that this experience would bring was exhilarating. She would trust. That was the answer, trust. She would hang loose, let be what will be and trust God to ride the waves along with her even should they become a tsunami. Liesl took a deep breath then headed out to walk the starboard deck where she hoped to spend hours meditating and discovering.

Liesl had never been afraid of change or new experiences. She never knew a new challenge that couldn't be named "adventure." She hoped that the voyage she was about to embark on would bring her to the work she had sought all these years, since she was a teenager.

* * *

Binh's Grandfather continued the story. "Priscilla Clause was Allie's mother. Both of them were on this ship. This voyage was a gift from Allie to her mom, one she felt was long overdue, but it turned out to be Allie who was most gifted by the voyage."

* * *

Chapter 6

ALLIE and PRISCILLA

When Allie first heard that her mom, Priscilla, only sixty-nine years old, was showing early signs of dementia, her first thought was to take her to see Eddie her son, and her German grandchildren. She wanted to give her mom, not only the care but also the friendship that only she could give. There is a reason for everything, she had been taught. She didn't really believe that, but maybe it was a truth, forcing itself on her now. Maybe this was the reason she had never married. Allie's sense of responsibility for her mom Priscilla, dated back to her childhood.

Priscilla did not grow up in a coal mining town. She was a midwestern girl. She had met Alex during high school days when he came to Wisconsin for a summer to help on his uncle's farm. Priscilla and Alex had ended up at the same barnyard dance one night and danced right into each others hearts. When Alex wrote to Priscilla inviting her to visit him in his home town of Plentiful, West Virginia she jumped from her chair with his letter in hand and ran to her Dad with the announcement, "I think he might want to marry me." Priscilla called the train station for a reservation and was headed out of town to Plentiful, WV the next week.

At nineteen Priscilla could not imagine that there was anything that love could not conquer. Although Alex had been hired to work in the local coal mine, she knew she would and could wait every day of her lifetime until he walked in the back door, blue eyes and white teeth shining out from a soot covered face and black curly dust-filled hair.

In the long run she was right. She did love her Alex enough, but the worry lines started to appear on her forehead too young. She longed for a child who would look like him. In her heart, though she couldn't bring herself to say it to Alex, she knew, that if that mine ever exploded she wanted his perfect image in his child to remind her of him. Priscilla's and Alex's first two children were boys but with their straight blond hair and brown eyes, were better matches of herself than of him. Then, when their little girl was born, Priscilla took one look at the black curly hair and squinty blue eyes and her cheeks, already dimpled, and knew she had to name her Alexis. Alexis quickly became

Allie when the child came crawling to her every time Priscilla called Alex.

Allie was like her father in other ways too, her appearance being only a hint of their real twinship. She followed him everyplace. By the time Allie was ten, she sported not only his looks, but his generosity, his responsibility, his spontaneous acceptance of all kinds of people, his effervescence and devilishness. Both tomboy and prissy lady, she climbed trees and played with make-up. She baby sat, cooked dinner and disappeared to the swimming hole when she had enough of chores.

Allie was swinging on the front porch swing which hung from two chains that Alex had taught the boys to hang, when Priscilla called her to come in. "Daddy will be home soon and I need help with dinner. Will you do the corn fritters, please."

As she stood over the stove with pancake turner in hand, humming and doing a little jig to "Alexander's Ragtime Band," Allie saw Daddy coming up the walk. She'd like to run out to hug him home but couldn't drop the spatula quickly enough. He caught the screen door behind him as he entered.

"Hey Little A" he called her by his favorite pet name for her. Allie smiled ear to ear, or rather pigtail to pigtail, as he leaned over and gave her a peck on the cheek, picked up her tune and rhythm and headed into the bathroom to wash off the coal soot.

Priscilla stopped off at the bathroom as she returned to the kitchen, to give Alex a kiss on the back of his head. "How was the coal today? and how is my coal king?" she asked. Her footstep was lighter once he arrived home.

Alex turned around and caught Priscilla with his lips that were now, not only black with soot but also wet. "Hey Miss Prissy. If the king is dirty the queen should be too. I love you Miss Prissy."

Wiping the coal but not the smile off her face, Priscilla stepped onto the porch and rang her big cow bell to call the family to dinner. Eddie and Rick ran up the steps and in the screen door letting it slam. Alex called them back. "Rick, open the door again and close it gently," he demanded. "He squirted me with his pen,"Rick yelled as he reappeared rubbing his black smudged face clean with his shirt sleeve, then obediently opening and closing the screen door.

Once they were all seated Alex prayed. "Dear Father, we thank you that we are all here together this evening, and thank you for the food on our table," he prayed, as Priscilla slapped Eddie's elbow off the table. This was Priscilla's favorite time, all of them together for another evening. She prayed that it would be that way for many years to come.

It was the very next day that the siren from the mine began to scream at ten o'clock in the morning. Silent panic spread throughout the town. Ma and Pa, Alex's parents, headed straight for the mine knowing Priscilla would already be there. The vigil of the entire town had begun. The kids were sent home to sleep during the night, though they didn't sleep, but were allowed to keep vigil with their parents during the day. The twenty-two families whose fathers, sons, husbands and brothers were in the mine, all hung out at the entrance to the mine and watched as the rescue team worked.

For a while hope rose when Mr. Lewis came out of the mine to get air and water. "I think the men are getting air through little tunnels and pockets I can see in the coal." Then hope fell. Little John Thompson, grown up to sixteen years old now and allowed to work on the rescue team, came from the mine for a break. He had been working almost twenty-four hours straight. "I can hardly breathe down there," he said, not understanding what those few words meant to the waiting family members. Townspeople who had no relatives in the mine made pilgrimages with sandwiches and coffee to those who were waiting.

It took forty-eight horrible hours. Friday afternoon the workers brought up the first stretcher bearing Mr. Avery. He was dead. Other families' members began sobbing. Priscilla stunned, stared into space, then after a moment noticed Mrs. Avery standing alone in shock. She straightened her own weak knees and went to Mrs. Avery's side, becoming herself, a brace for Mrs Avery. She stood with her arm around that grieving woman for a long time, maybe it was several hours. Mrs. Avery would not leave the site until she knew the rest of the story even though she now knew that her own husband of thirty-five years was dead. One body after another was carried from the mine. Priscilla's Alex was number twelve.

Alex's Ma and Pa were at Priscilla's side. Before taking Priscilla and the children home, they dropped off Mrs. Avery who insisted that she be taken to her own home though she knew she'd be there alone.

Sadness and grief were the only things plentiful in the emotion-shattered town that year. Not wanting to uproot her children from their grandparents, friends, school and the only town they knew, Priscilla remained in Plentiful, but she depended more and more upon Allie, as she was growing older, for companionship. She was determined that her children had to live for the future. With Ma and Pa's help, her boys would not work in the coal mine and her daughter would find a way out of town so as not to fall in love with a miner.

How fast seven years go when you watch your little ones grow into adulthood even if you have a big black hole in your own heart. How slow it passes when you are ten and want to be an adult. But a day did come in May, 1950. It was already summer although only spring by the calendar. The sky was dark and Priscilla and Allie sat on the wooden steps and watched the bugs dance around the porch light. This was the time Allie had chosen to speak to her mom, to have that painful conversation that had to happen sometime. She felt almost in a panic and had to force herself to bring out the first words, knowing that her mom would help her get the rest out.

"Mamma, when I graduate..."

Priscilla's heart fell into her stomach. Here it is, that moment she had dreaded. She was soon to lose Alexis who had become like a best friend to her. If she ever had to be brave, it was now.

"Do you suppose I could get a job at the Woolworth in Gary? Then I could move to town..."

Priscilla knew that Allie did not dream of a career at the Woolworth in Gary. She was adventurous despite the grounded life into which she was born. It was time for her to fly away, to fill her lungs full of new air.

"Alexis you don't have to stay close by. I know you've got it all thought out, how to protect me." Priscilla hesitated between each phrase to let it sink in and also, to swallow the tears that would surely choke her if she didn't. "Allie, when I was your age I followed my dreams. When I decided to move here to Plentiful with Dad everyone said I was wrong, that I didn't know what I wanted at nineteen years of age. But you know, I was right. Even if I had known how I'd lose your father, I would have made the same choice. Sometimes our dreams don't turn out the way we dreamt them, but still we are richer because of them and they shape our possibilities and help us choose a direction."

They sat in silence for a long time. Allie fought back the tears that can only come from hurting someone you love. She looked at the bugs in the yellow porch light, not able to look her mom in the eyes.

She couldn't speak and didn't know what to say. Priscilla finally spoke again.

"One of the reasons I would have made the choice I made to move to Plentiful and marry Daddy, is you. That choice gave us you. You know, your dad would have died whether or not he had me. Without the courage, or maybe the fool hardiness of that choice of mine he would still be dead now. But he is not dead. He lives in your blue eyes and black curls and in your loyalty. And he can live in your adventure."

In the tears that Allie could not fight back now, her mother read her sadness at the possibility of their parting. It seemed to Allie that her mom's mind was made up. Her mother's determination was freeing and made the decision to leave just a little easier. After an eternal minute Priscilla spoke again. "Allie, when your Aunt Kitty moved to California we felt sorry for her, thinking she would be so alone. But she dreamt of oranges and sunshine and the Pacific Ocean and said someday we'd be glad she was there so we'd have an excuse to visit. But there's a reason for everything. Kitty is still alone. I bet she would love to have you stay with her for awhile so you could get a job and maybe go to school."

No, dreams do not always turn out the way we dreamt them, Priscilla thought. Reality, not dreams, took Alex from us. Reality has beckoned Eddie to the Air Force and is now reaching for Alexis. Priscilla stretched out her generous arms to send her child away, knowing that if or when she returned it would not be as her little girl but as a peer woman, maybe with babes of her own.

Kitty loved the idea of having Allie live with her. During the next three months, while Priscilla and Alexis were planning, buying, packing and visiting in preparation for her departure, Kitty was researching day and night schools and job opportunities in her town of Santa Barbara. Priscilla bought train tickets for them both, a one-way for Allie and a round trip ticket for herself. Looking forward to the adventure of her trip to California and a great time with her sister in Santa Barbara, helped Priscilla get ready for the grief of sending Allie off. When together, they heard the conductor sing "All aboard," they were both ready for Allie's new start in life.

Priscilla's dream to see her children escape the coal mines, was fulfilled over the years. Ricky for a short time had a job in the coal mine of Plentiful but soon he realized that he wanted to work where he could see brother sun shine. He loved the farm hand job he had found and piece-by-piece, was buying his own land. Eddie joined the Air Force and married Margit Koch, a German girl from Diessen, an idyllic fishing village that he had made his home.

After graduating from the University of California, Santa Barbara, Allie had obtained a job as a gofer at the Aeronautics Research Site in San Luis Obispo, California.

Alexis's work had always been an adventure for her. Work was her life. Now at thirty-seven, she needed to keep her job. She had plied her way in the aerospace industry by continuing her schooling in science engineering and astronomy while she worked her way up from an entry level position. What other job, or what man for that matter, could provide the excitement she experienced when she successfully designed the flag that would be placed on the moon by the astronauts of Apollo 11 and the material for their suits? Even though Allie had thought she wanted to marry, she now felt that at her age, family life was no longer a choice for her.

Suddenly, Alexis was faced with a decision she had never even considered having to make. When Rick called to tell her of her mom's diagnosis, Alzheimer's Disease, she had to hang up the phone and call him back. She was mute of a response.

"Rick, what can we do for her? Can she stay alone any longer? Can she live with you on the farm? How would I manage her if she came out here? Do I need to take a leave of absence?"

Then Eddie came up with the perfect solution. "Margit wants Mom to come and stay with us a while in Diessen so our children can get to know her before its too late for them. Is there any way we can manage that?" he asked.

"How can we possibly get her to Germany?" was the immediate reaction of both Rick and Alexis. Then Alexis started to think about Eddie's idea and investigate. It wouldn't be easy. Travel might only confuse Mom more. A freight ship should be a good option though. It would be calmer than a passenger ship and there would be only a few people with whom Priscilla would have to interact. After working fifteen years at the Research Institute, Alexis had accumulated months of vacation time and if needed would be allowed a leave of absence to be with her mother. Finally all of the kids and in-laws agreed that it was the perfect plan.

Eddie assured the others that Diessen had the best medical care available anyplace, for the elderly. Allie and Eddie planned to determine later, if it would be best for their mom to stay with him and Margit and the three kids in Diessen so that Allie could get back to work, or whether Priscilla should return to America with Allie. Allie already had her own return ticket purchased for three months from departure day.

The day came and Alexis had arranged for her vacation and possible leave of absence. Rick brought their mom to San Francisco where they met Alexis at the St. Francis Hotel. The three of them stayed at the hotel for a few days before Rick caught a return train and Allie made ready for the next day's departure on the California Bear. "Mom, I have all of your things packed and ready. Will you sit here and watch me while I pack my things?"

"Alexis, maybe I shouldn't go with you." Priscilla frowned.

"Mom, you want to see Eddie and the kids, I know. And I will show you my favorite stars from the ship. You've always wanted to see them with me."

"Can we go by train instead? I really enjoyed the train ride."

"When we get off the ship in Rotterdam, Holland, we'll take a train to Eddie's house and you'll see Margit and your three grandchildren. You will love the trip Mom, and I'll be with you the whole time."

"Okay, lets go. I'll get my purse."

"We're going tomorrow, Mom. I laid out your new jeans, your yellow sweater and brown loafers for you to wear. Why don't you look them over and see if they're okay, while I get my things ready. We'll leave for the ship at 4:00 tomorrow afternoon." Alexis knew she'd have to tell her this many times by 4:00 and planned to leave earlier to walk around the dock with her in order to shorten the wait.

Surprisingly, Ricky had been able to bring his mom to California on the Zephyr without a hitch. She still seemed to enjoy travel. So on June twenty-second when Allie finally got her into a taxi heading for the dock, Priscilla was ready to go. She looked younger than her sixty-nine years in her slim-line jeans and yellow sweater with hair that had barely started turning grey. Her gait was still steady, feet straight ahead. She clutched her purse as she walked up the gangplank.

Luggage already in their cabin, Alexis was free to take her mother by the arm, but Priscilla resisted. "I can walk alone, Allie. You just follow me," she said.

Allie honored her desire for independence and would be there if needed. She made her way up the ramp behind her mom. She was wearing black tight fitting jeans and black sandals. Her starched white blouse and bright aqua sport jacket complemented her still curly like her dad's, but no longer braided black hair and blue eyes. At the top of the ramp, she greeted Beverly with a firm handshake. Beverly was left speechless for the first time by this attractive pair of women entering her domain. Priscilla and Allie made their way to the lounge and found their cabin, between that of John and Daiki and that of Don. They were the last to board. Excitement was brewing now.

* * *

"I still have to tell you about Beverly, Ethel and John, the one we called 'Goose.' But I must get on with the story. You'll hear more about them as we tell you the whole story," Grandma said. Binh's grandparents were concerned about his time. They wanted very much to finish their story before he had to leave for the Armstrong Space Center for his launch.

* * *

Chapter 7

DEPARTURE

Don and Goose bumped into each other on the eighth level of the ship as they were about to head down the stairway. When they introduced themselves to each other they both immediately knew they were meeting a kindred spirit.

"What brought you to traveling with cargo?" Don had asked Goose.

"Hain't no sense settin' in a chair flyin' over them waters when you can ride the waves and feel the world you're livin' in."

Could it be? "Goose"? Surely that's not his real name, Don wondered. And he sounds a little like Johnny Cash he thought. This might not be such a boring trip after all.

It was almost 7:00 when they met. From their view on the top deck, it looked like the hold was closed and there was little activity at dock side which probably meant they would depart on time. The gangway planks had been raised. Don and Goose were the last to reach the fourth level where the passengers gathered to wave to the few people who were at the boat side to send them off. What an exciting time for the eleven. In addition to the separate venture that each of them proposed to themselves, they were also about to become housemates with the other ten, with whom they would be spending the next four to eight weeks depending on their point of disembarking. The activity and mood on board though celebratory, was more like adults in parallel play than like a party of friends, or a gathering of people with something in common.

Ethel and Liesl were waving to four of their religious Sisters who lived in San Francisco and had come to see them off. The Sisters at dock side were talking with strangers. There were always some people who came to watch ships set sail. These were shaking their heads in amazement at the Sisters' tale. Lillian's family was there en masse, the children jumping with excitement, the adults crying. Don while enjoying Goose's conversation, glanced cautiously at the onlookers, greatly relieved to see that his parents were not here. Priscilla and Allie made it to dockside of the ship on time. They stood together but Priscilla made it clear that she did not want Allie's arm around her. "I can wave and hold on like everyone else, " she said. Debra, Barry, Daiki and Beverly waived heartily at the anonymous gathering. The Bear like an impatient duck gave five loud honks and the ship, led by a little tug boat edged slowly away from the dock. The people on shore got smaller and smaller. There was a thirty second silence while Lillian became teary, Liesl, ignoring all rules, took off and waived her veil, Daiki high-fived Barry who was standing next to him, then Goose spoke up,

"Better be gettin' fore if ya wanna see the Golden Gate when we cross under her. Ya don't wanna miss her fer not knowin' what to do."

All the passengers suddenly seeming to realize that they were in this together, smiled at each other and turned to follow Goose who apparently knew what to do next.

They reached the rail at the bow in time to see the sun hitting the bridge and changing its gold into orange. The passengers were turning and gawking, trying to get a 360 degree view that they'd never forget. The sky which had been baby blue all day was now French grey-blue, the water was sparkling. They were totally awestruck and silent. Don, standing next to Liesl, gazed at the horizon. His eyes met Liesl's sparkling like the water, the orange sun setting her face on fire. He was unfamiliar with nuns but he thought at that moment that she was the most beautiful woman he had ever seen. On this enchanted evening he was seeing his stranger. He was abashed. Didn't know what to say to her, yet knew he wouldn't let her go. He smiled at her sheepishly. The warmth of her return smile was like a hot shower on a cold day; but why did she look away so quickly after catching his eye? Was she feeling drawn to him too?

Liesl quickly turned away from Don's easy smile to watch the ripples on the water made by the ship. She was aware of that feeling of fancy for a man that always prodded her to turn away quickly, to remove herself from a situation.

This time Liesl stayed surveying the ocean until the sun was gone. When nature's show seemed to be finished, it started all over again showing off its thousands of milky ways. When Liesl couldn't absorb any more beauty, she returned to the room she shared with Ethel. After arranging her belongings in the room she lay down, so elated she thought she'd never get to sleep. The ship rocked ever so gently on the calm sea and soon she did fall asleep, dreaming for the first time in her life, of being rocked in the arms of a man. The man of her dream happened to have a mustache and wavy auburn hair.

Chapter 8

SEASCAPE

The passengers had been instructed to meet in their lounge after breakfast for some further information and instructions about their journey. In the early morning Liesl jumped up to watch the sun from her porthole. She could hardly tear herself away from the view. As she looked out at the sea and sky, she remembered her dream. Then her thoughts turned to the silent visual exchange with Don the previous evening. It made her nervous. She had better avoid too much contact with Don. Her attraction could spell trouble. Nothing was to distract her from her mission, a life belonging to God in the service of the poor.

Debra watched the sunrise from the eighth deck of the ship, totally in awe. She had promised herself an hour of meditation every morning but was too amazed at the view to even think about her own breathing. Daiki also planned to watch the sunrise from the top deck but when he reached there and saw Debra in lotus position he felt a reverence for her that he didn't want to disturb, so he turned back to the lounge. Lillian was in the lounge, silently putting together her little wooden easel. Goose was there watching Lillian with interest. All but Beverly managed to arrive by the time the sun had risen over the waters. The buildings on the California shore were no longer in sight.

Again, with no formal directions, Goose took over. "Y'all want somethin to eat, ya better head on out to the dining room."

They all followed Goose for their first breakfast on board, Beverly having joined the group. Just down the deck from the lounge they found a small dining room with three card-table sized tables set with linen cloth, sparkling clear water glasses, real silverware. Except for the absence of little vases of flowers, it reminded Liesl of the diner on the Southern Pacific she once rode across country with her grandparents.

Liesl and Ethel sat at the table with Debra and Barry. When they were all seated, the steward entered, asked each for their choice of drinks. He returned with silver coffee pot and crystal pitchers of water and orange juice. After serving the drinks he began carrying on his shoulder, trays of sausage, bacon, anchovies, scrambled eggs, various bread baskets, bowls of rice and of fruit and placed them on each table. All the passengers ate heartily but the conversation was muted as with strangers trying to make polite conversation. The steward announced that Captain Mack would like to meet with the passengers in the lounge at 0900 hours to give them information and that they were all free until that time.

At 9:00 sharp, Captain Mack arrived in the lounge. Everyone quieted and found seating.

"Hi everyone. I'm Captain Mack Engle. You are all very welcome joining the crew for our voyage around the world. However, you will not be mixing with the crew. They are here working and have very busy and important duties keeping you safe and delivering cargo to many countries around the world. In addition you are aware that we will be sailing into some unfriendly territories. It is important that the crew have their mind on their duties and is not distracted by repartee with passengers. You are requested to comply with this limitation. You will rarely even see crew members except for me. A bursar will be available to you after this meeting and at each port, in case you want to lock up money or valuables.

Meals will be served in the passengers' dining room at 0700, 1300 and 1800. You are expected to be there at these times as there will be no other food provided. You will have assigned seating from now on and will be expected to sit at the same table for every meal. Since there are only eleven of you there is one extra chair at the three tables. I will often be eating with you so I will occupy the empty place or move one of you.

Tomorrow, when we are well underway, I will provide a tour of the ship for anyone interested. You are free to roam this deck as well as the sixth level deck and to take the steps to the eighth level. Please do not go to the lower levels at any time as this is sleeping and eating quarters and work space for crew. The four lowest levels carry cargo. The engine and boiler rooms are in the bottom level. Are there any questions?

"What do we do if we need something?

"Beverly, there is an intercom system which you could use to access me in a real emergency. Your access to it is from the dining room and I will show it to you when we leave here. Remember however this is only for a real emergency. We have no medical staff on board. You all know that you are expected to have all medical supplies that you may need in your own possession. We do have first aid services provided by one of our sailors who is a medic. You may help each other of course. The Good Samaritan Law applies on board. Just use common sense.

"One more thing. For the next six days, each day will be twenty-five hours long. We make this change in time at 1800 hours each day. When you go to dinner each evening it will be 1800. After an hour in the dining room you will adjust your watches from 1900 back to 1800. Then on the seventh day, when we cross the International Date Line, we will skip an entire day so that the date and time will be correct when we reach land in Japan.

"I'm sure you are all aware that there is no communication with land available for you for about eight days while we are crossing. I hope you all enjoy your journey across the Pacific Ocean."

With that abrupt farewell, Captain Mack turned and left the lounge.

The passengers looked at each other briefly, then started to change positions, some to walk out to the deck, some to pick up a magazine or to return to their own quarters. Liesl walked out onto the aft deck to watch the albatross following the ship. As she was leaning on the rail, Don approached and leaned next to her. He was again wearing his jeans and sneakers but now was wearing a green flannel shirt that accented the color of his eyes.

"An amazing sight," he said. "I feel like the Ancient Mariner."

At the warmth of his closeness, Liesl felt the stirring that she had feared in the early morning.

"You don't look ancient to me, but you do look like I picture a mariner," she said, looking for words to hide her turmoil. They stood closely and wordlessly side by side for several minutes, Don wanting to be close, Liesl pretending to herself that she didn't. Suddenly Ethel appeared between them.

"Thought you might want to join us for a game of cards," she said to them both. It was the last thing either of them wanted but they both acquiesced. There was time. There would be a lot of time in the next four weeks. When they reached the lounge, Lillian, Alexis,

Priscilla, Barry and Goose were at the lone table and had made space for three more chairs. "Ever hear of six handed poker?" Lillian asked.

Goose put his arm around Priscilla. "You and I will sit out the first game," he said to her. "I don't know how to play this and anyhowse, I'd rather flirt with you while I learn." Priscilla smiled and did a "pshaw" with her hand. Allie was pleased at the way Goose had picked up on her mom's need so quickly and how he had managed to make her feel good about the arrangement.

* * *

Thus began their voyage in that boring room where nothing important could happen. "They sat in that same lounge, the eleven of them, for hours each day. Most of them were not board game players, yet as they played those silly games, they laughed and hee-hawed and ribbed each other for hours on end. They had Ethel to thank for the games and cards and Liesel for the guitar and song sheets. The other passengers had packed only the things they expected to need for themselves, except Lillian of course, who brought all those things for the kids in Asia. Although the others didn't bring things for them to do, they each brought themselves to the table, a vast assortment of good cheer. There was no recluse on this ship and no one's gladness or sadness went unnoticed. They all learned from necessity, how important friendship was. Even Beverly who was always the odd man out, was important to the whole. They were a tangible example of variety being life's spice.

When the ding-a-ling rang to announce lunch at 1300 on that first day, they were all surprised at how fast the time had passed. They arrived in the dining room to find the tables, again exquisitely set, but this time there were name plates at each place. The first table was set for Debra, Barry, Lillian and Beverly. The second was labeled Priscilla, Alexis, John and Daiki and the third, Liesl, Ethel and Don. These would be permanent table partners.

Liesl felt flustered. She knew she would enjoy Don's company, but keeping her distance would be difficult if they ate all of their meals together. Ethel would be even more difficult. She must have already noticed Don's attraction to Liesl, or at least it seemed that way when she came barging in between them that morning as they stood together looking out at the water. Well she didn't have to worry. They weren't going to play footsies at the dining room table. Besides, Liesl had her own decision to honor, didn't need someone else's supervising conscience.

Each passenger was experiencing some kind of reaction to their table assignment. Debra and Beverly eyed each other suspiciously; Allie and Goose giggled like children in each others' presence, but none questioned or made any attempt to change their place.

As the second day dawned, they all started to fall into the patterns they had in their everyday lives. Daiki had asked Debra if she minded him being present on the eighth deck in the early morning. "I promise not to disturb you" he assured her. "In fact, I will sit at the other end of the ship from you. I, too, want to start my day with meditation. I've been doing this all my life. It helps me to be peaceful with anything that happens to me during the day."

And so, Debra and Daiki were on the eighth deck by 4:30 the next morning. Ethel felt that she and Liesl should begin each morning with prayer in the privacy of their cabin. Don, Barry and Goose walked the deck alone but passed each other in their walking, big smiles showing their pleasure at being alone. Lillian tiptoed out of her room to avoid waking Beverly, then found a comfortable chair on the fourth deck for watching the sunrise.

At breakfast Captain Mack stopped in the dining room to remind the passengers that there would be a tour of the ship at 1000 hours. All were eagerly waiting in the lounge when he arrived at ten o'clock sharp.

"I'll be taking you to the boiler room first. That is the very bottom of the ship and is off limits except for this time, with me. Be sure that you stay with me. No one is to wander off in that area because it is dangerous. It will be noisy. If you can't hear my explanation hold your questions until we come back up from there. You are not to interrupt the crew that you will see."

The passengers all followed Captain Mack closely, excited to be taken down a rickety elevator with cable hoists to the bowels of the ship. It was a cool morning so they were all wearing heavy clothes or sweaters. The engine room was hot. Except for their wonder at the size and the noise of the steam boilers and the electric generator, there was no reason to hang out there. They were glad to climb the steps to the third level where they could snoop around to see what the crew's quarters were like.

They couldn't see much except that a few doors were open. Their quarters were similar to the passengers' with private or two-man rooms, each with grey woolen blankets on single beds. They were all neat. There must have been rules about making beds and picking up after themselves before starting their day. Like being in the navy. The few doors on the third level that they could see were marked, "Doctor's room," "Purser's room," "Fireman's room" and "Boy's room." "Who is the boy?" Beverly asked everybody or nobody. And nobody answered, just shrugged.

It was a long walk to the steering room in the front of the main deck of the ship. It was so pretty in the steering room, windows all the way around, with a huge brass steering wheel and mahogany console in the middle. Even the walls and window frames were mahogany. The ship was actually being steered at the moment by Pilot Mahoney. He was dressed in a navy colored double breasted suit with gold colored trim on his sleeve cuffs and wore a white "captain's cap." He made them feel they were in good hands, a real professional steering their ship.

"This is Pilot Mahoney," Captain Mack introduced.

"How do you do folks." Pilot Mahoney continued looking forward, rapt in whatever he was seeing or thinking about. Or maybe he was thinking about looking rapt, so that he wouldn't have to interact with the passengers.

"His job is the most important on the ship..."

"Except for you." Beverly interrupted.

"No, including me. It is the pilot's job to keep up with weather reports..."

"Sure hope he's better than our weather man," again from Beverly.

"Beverly, one of his jobs is to give the crew directions. If you don't let me finish I will assign you to the pilot to receive your directions from him."

Beverly did not seem at all embarrassed as she turned and smiled sheepishly at the other passengers. Lillian reached out warmly and took her by the arm.

"Stay back here with me Bev." She took Beverly's arm and warmly guided her to her side.

"To do his job the pilot must understand all the navigation equipment, both the new technology systems and procedures and the ancient ones. Our crew still navigates the ship by the stars at night and switches to automatic in the daylight but if either system fails, it is the pilot's job to substitute. He operates the radios, communicates with other vessels and lighthouses, navigates harbors, steers us into our berths, docks and undocks our ship, sets our course around reefs and shoals, and icebergs, maintains logs, oversees cargo storage below deck and is responsible for rescue missions.

"Oh, rescue..."

Lillian shook Beverly's arm. It stopped her immediately, from some ungodly hysterical remark about the Titanic.

"We are traveling one degree south of our planned route," Pilot Mahoney said. "This is because the water temperature is colder than we estimated. However, in warmer water the speed drops slightly. This and the fact that the more southern, straighter route is slightly longer, may cause us to reach Yokohama later than planned. Any questions?"

"How can straighter be longer?" Barry asked.

Pilot Mahoney pulled a globe out from under his dashboard. He must have been asked this question before. Always the educator, he was ready to demonstrate. "Look at the shape of the earth. Now, draw a line from the west coast of America, to Japan" He demonstrated with his finger. "If I draw the line straight west, I am drawing it near the center of the globe were it is at the globe's largest part. Now if I move my finger several degrees further north and cross at a more northern latitude the line is shorter because it curves the smaller part of the globe. It is further from the equator. In nature, a straight line is not always the shortest distance between two points."

"Never thought of it that way," Barry said. "And here I thought, at twenty-four, I was too old to learn much more."

"Barry, you'd better learn something every day of your life or you're dead," Goose said. "Captain Mack, what else, you gonna teach us?"

"Come and see," Captain Mack said, leading them out onto the deck. They acquired a new understanding of the equipment that they had been seeing all along. The huge derricks, booms, masts were all for the purpose of loading and unloading freight. There were also antennas to pick up communication. They saw the huge funnels, the smokestacks that expel the steam from the boilers they had seen in the engine room. Their ship had four funnels painted bright red and black.

Seeing their ship was so interesting that they forgot to look at their watches and were surprised when Captain Mack said, "Lets go to lunch, I'll join you today." He joined the table with Liesl, Ethel and Don. He answered their questions all through lunch, mostly about the lives of sailors, their ages, length of service, families. For most of the passengers this lunch was also a new food experience: dried squid, seaweed and the slurping of noodles. They laughed a lot as they practiced slurping. "Our mom would have spanked us for this," Barry said to Debra, wiping his chin.

As they left the table, Lillian caught Beverly winking at Mack. He kept his gaze in the direction he was walking as if he didn't notice her. Lillian returned to her room for a nap. Expecting Beverly to come in for a discussion of the morning, she lay awake waiting, but finally dozed off. When she awoke she looked out to the lounge, but no Beverly. Then, she entered her bathroom and was there several minutes. When she was coming out of their bathroom she opened the door to find Beverly on her knees reaching under her bed. Lillian pulled back into the bathroom without being noticed by Beverly. She waited there for two minutes. When it seemed that all was clear, Beverly, gone from their cabin, she joined the others in the lounge.

A hand of poker had just finished. Goose stretched out his arms above his head. "I need to get up and walk around," he said. "Need some exercise."

"Good Goose!" Daiki said. "Goose, I've been hoping you'd let me interview you." Can I walk with you and do that now?"

Chapter 9

GOOSE

"Interview me?" Goose was flabbergasted. "I haint got much to tell you about me. I just been a sailor since I was walkin up to thirteen years old. No need to interview me, just tell me what you want to know. I don't hide my teeth, but I don't know too much either.

"Well Goose, first, before we go out, tell me, tell all of us, how you got the name "Goose."

"I can tell you that, easy. How would you like to be called 'Jack Ash', accent on the Jack? That's what them kids in Tennessee called me. Boy, they liked making Jack Ash out of my name John since my last name is Ash. So's when I got to my first ship job I didn't tell em sailors my real name. So one guy said 'You'll be just like them albatross always following a ship. We'll just call you 'Albatross.' After they saw me work though, one guy says, 'He ain't no follower, you cain't call him albatross. He's more like the lead goose that heads up that "V" when the geese fly.' So they called me 'Goose' that morning and that name stuck. I kinda like it."

"So do I," Don laughed as the others shook their heads in approval.

"Well, come on Daiki, lets take a hike and get to that interviewing you're after."

Daiki and Goose stepped out onto the deck and were glad to be wearing jackets. Although the sun was bright, the wind was mighty fore to aft. The ocean water sprayed and the wind blew into their faces and blew Daiki's buttons open. They decided to turn around. Now his straight black hair blew over his eyes. They found a sheltered spot at the rear outside the passenger quarters and sat.

"Well, here goes," said Goose. "All about me. I was twelve when my Paw didn't come back from sea. He was a sailor like me. Ma never said if he had an accident or if he died of some disease, maybe picked up from one of them women in some port. Anyway she said they buried him out there in the ocean. Then she went to other folks' houses to scrub and cook and care for them's young uns. I was the man then, the only one. Ma had five girls after me. Heck who wants to be paw to five girls. 'Jack can I stay home from school today?' 'Jack, can I go dancing tonight?' Jack was supposed to change diapers and haul babes around and cook. I couldn't do it no more so's I went to sea like Paw. Ma didn't like it. Meant Lily Sue had to take over. I respected my ma but every bird has to leave the nest sometime.

"I told the captain I was sixteen but he didn't ask me for proof. I was already five foot nine and strong as Crocket himself from hackin and haulin wood, so I could haul those sacks of rice or sugar like none of them older men. Heck, gimme a barge load of tree trunks and I'd get it loaded while the other men were trying to figure out how to lift a log."

Daiki had planned to take notes but was so fascinated that he forgot to write. When he remembered, he was afraid to interrupt Goose's rambling so he tried to get the flavor instead of the peas and carrots of the conversation. "Ever been married?" Daiki asked.

"Heck no. Got lots of pretty girls in every port. I like it that way. They all laugh when I come, cry when I go and hanker when I'm gone."

"Ever go to school?"

"Now that's a question I hain't know how to answer. Me and Lily Sue hiked to the school house about four years, enough to learn me how to read. Reading's all I needed to set me to learning myself. Heck, I know all them poets and history and geography better than school can teach you. Bobby and Lizzy Browning: 'How do I love thee?', Longfellow: 'Listen my children and you will hear', Leo Tolstoy: 'Ivan, everybody dies someday' and my favorite: from Robert Blake: 'Hold infinity in the palm of your hand and eternity in an hour'. But education, heck I seen my own Antonia, and almost every ship's got its own Huck Finn. Guess them books and live people give me all the education anybody could ask for."

"Goose, why are you going to the Philippines on this trip?"

"Like I said, I got a girl everyplace and this one's worth seeing. She come down to the ship when I was sailing. She'd brung a truck load of books whenever we docked. When I read them all, I'd leave them at the next port and get replacements. What could I do on the ship when I had a day off cept sit on my arse. Might as well read myself into other worlds.

"If the ship has been your whole life, how come you retired from shipping?" Daiki thought Goose was the kind to work til he couldn't any more.

"Now that there's a good question. I saw those young uns getting jobs. They can lift more than me now. Besides they need work more than me. I got all the means I need socked away now. Sides, If I don't get paid for going, I can go where I want, live free."

"Goose, one last question; have you ever been on drugs?"

"Heck no. Coulda been. Port hogs always wanta sell them. But me, I like seeing the real sea and sky and knowing real folks, not them ones that come to haunt you when you're high.

"Is that all you want to know, Daiki? See, you don't need no interview. I'll tell you whatever you want to know. Let's go back inside, its gettin mighty cold."

As they were walking back toward the lounge, Goose, too, had to lean into the wind, hold his jacket closed, his arms folded against his chest, the waves in his brown hair blown straight.

"Ain't those some women we got on this ship, Daiki? he said. Especially that Allie! Just imagine, she's been studying the stars and planets most of her life. I think she's a real astronomer. Someday you should interview her. Now that would be some interview for you."

The men returned to their room, Goose to lie down and think about what he had just said about Allie, Daiki to make notes before he would forget anything that Goose had told him. Daiki wanted to capture Goose's philosophy, mannerisms, words, history, his whole life. And Goose, well as he thought about it, he might have something to capture too.

Chapter 10

LIESL AND DON

Lillian seemed to be alone. She checked the lounge, her room, her bathroom. No Beverly. Quickly she returned to her room and got down on her knees. Better hurry, getting up off her knees wasn't so quick anymore. She lifted the skirt of Beverly's bed. There was the secret, a liquor box, half full of liquor, a scotch, a bourbon, a brandy all unopened. Had Beverly boarded the vessel with the liquor? She had been the first one to board. Or was she getting it from someone on the ship? She did disappear frequently, everyone had noticed that. They all needed some time alone, out of that "mental-hospital-lounge", they all agreed. They had figured that Beverly had found herself a spot to hide; but then, it wasn't like Beverly to want to be alone.

Lillian held on to the bedside stand to pull herself up. She straightened Beverly's bed skirt and quilt so that her surreptitious intrusion into Beverly's life wouldn't be noticed. For now she would just watch Beverly and not say anything about her find. Where did Beverly go when she was gone? Now Lillian was more curious than ever about her roomy's behavior.

Lillian returned quickly to the lounge and found Don there alone. Her secret just bubbled out. She couldn't help herself. "Don, what do you suppose Beverly does when she's alone? Don't tell anyone, but I found a box of liquor under her bed."

"I don't know where she goes, Lillian," Don said, "but she does know how to get to Captain Mack's quarters. She showed me the way when I boarded. But think about it Lillian. She needs all the help she can get to lighten her spirit a little. I wouldn't interfere for anything, with a little fun she might be having."

"You're right Don." Lillian said. "I'm glad you're the person I told, because I know I can rely on you to keep quiet about it. I wouldn't want anyone to think I'm snooping or anything. If anything happens to her, or if she gets into trouble, you'd know what to do for her."

Don didn't want to participate in gossip about other passengers. He figured they all had their eccentricities and in fact, he was glad of it. He got up from the table and sauntered out of the lounge to the stairway. He needed a place to sit and think, not just about Beverly but about himself. He wanted to get a better handle on his feelings for Liesl. When he reached the eighth deck, a place to sit and think he had hoped, there again was Liesl, leaning over the rail watching the water. Don also wanted to talk with Liesl, alone, without Ethel constantly interrupting them, so he might be able to do that now. Ethel always seemed to be watching, to find a way to interfere when he was anywhere near Liesl.

He wanted to get to know Liesl better. He already knew her sense of values. How many young women wanted to go to Asia to help people with Leprosy? He already knew her sense of humor. Who else laughed when he described his family or when he slobbered his noodles? He knew her kindness. He had watched her converse with Priscilla and make Priscilla smile, even laugh. He knew, he really knew she stirred him, aroused him. When he looked at her he wanted to protect her, to hold her, to be closer. Their purposes on this journey seemed similar. Could they find a way to fulfill their missions together, he wondered?

Although he had come up here to be alone with his thoughts, Liesl standing there in the sea breeze, was like a magnet that pulled him over.

"Hi Liesl." he called as he approached, then waited. "What are you thinking about?" he asked when she didn't respond to his greeting.

Don leaned on the rail next to her; despite the cool and dampness from the sea, he could feel the heat of her body throughout his.

Liesl froze. Of course, she was thinking of Don, but she couldn't bring herself to tell him that. "I was thinking about our mission, mine and Ethel's I mean. You must think about your's a lot too. Where we're going we could be risking our lives and health. That doesn't frighten me at all though. There is something else that frightens me more. Liesl paused, her options racing through her mind. She wanted so much to confide in Don, yet from years of conviction and practice, could not let herself get so close to a man as to confide in him. If I just hold on a little longer I'll be in Thailand and he'll be in Vietnam. Our nearness will be over soon, she thought. I can do it. I can keep my distance.

But she couldn't. She took the first step. She confided. "Something else has been bothering me more than possible death though." She paused again, looking into his eyes, still not sure if he was the one with whom to share, trying to referee between her heart and her head.

"What is bothering you?" Don asked, studying her open face and cautious speech and demeanor as she gazed back at the ocean instead of at him.

As Liesl looked out into the deserted ocean waters, not even a seagull to distract them, she finally let her heart win. "I've been thinking that there is no one in my life who would suffer, who would even care or miss me if I was gone."

She got that wrong, Don thought. Already, he would care immensely, but this was the time for him to be still so that she would continue to vent.

She did. "I profess to love everyone, and that's not real. I mean if you love everyone equally, that's like loving no one...no one is special. The term, "Everyone" is too ethereal. It's too generic. There is no one person that I love enough to change my life for them. There may be a few people that would do that for me, but that's not good enough. It's only me that I can fix. It's me that needs to be more responsive to others. I'm the one who needs to decide if I should help someone, for example, go to my father and brothers when they need me. I need to be responsible for my own giving and receiving love."

"What has made you think about that all of a sudden, Liesl?" Don asked, hoping she could say, *"you Don, its living so many hours at your side that's making me think about it."* But she couldn't say it. Had she been brainwashed into thinking it was wrong to express her feelings? If so, how could he and Liesl get past years of fear in one or two months, before they had to separate from each other?

"I've been watching Barry and Debra," she finally responded thoughtfully. "When Barry took a leave of absence from his work, he took a chance on losing his whole career in order to help her. That's not how it has been with me. If I saw someone who needed help and my superior said, 'no, you can't take the time to help him, you need to come home now,' I would go home. Just that simple. I would ignore the needs of the other person to obey her.

"What kind of love is that? God's will? Hogwash. That's not even ordinary neighborliness." Liesl was angry. She was angry at herself for all those years she had listened to the pitch. "Feelings don't count." She had heard it over and over. She had been so sincere, so fooleartedly in love with God that she would do anything to please Him. And she had been told since she was a child, since the age of seventeen, that this would please Him. Told should be careful not to be too close to anyone. She should avoid being alone with a man. She was to avoid nearness even to her family, to avoid sharing a meal with them or calling or visiting them.

Now she was catching glimpses of a new reality. It might be time to listen to her heart. It might be time to listen to her Father in heaven tell her that it would please Him to see her fall in love with a person, with His plan in creating this wonderful world.

Don could see that Liesl was hurting but he couldn't interpret her feelings. He could see her hurt in her wet eyes and in the way she was so absorbed in her thoughts as she looked out at the deep blue of the sea and couldn't bring herself to look at him. Her cheeks were red and hot and her shoulders were squared. She looked ready for battle.

Liesl was experiencing a release from feelings she hadn't even known she had. She continued, "My parents and brothers have tried to love me. They have included me in everything that goes on in our family. But I haven't been there for them because I'm not allowed to be, and I've accepted that. I wasn't even allowed to be with my dad for my mom's funeral. So instead of loving someone specific I run around trying to save the world. That's not real love, is it? Its just my way of trying to make up for missing the real thing." Now Liesl's shoulders slumped and she leaned heavily on the rail.

Don had witnessed a purging of Liesl's pain, her much needed catharsis. He wanted to help her understand that she was not alone, and responded the best he knew how. "Liesl, your life has not been wasted. We all learn from experience what we couldn't know at seventeen. I'm not always sure that my motivation is so simple either. I too am willing to risk my life and limbs, but maybe not my own self-image. I've always thought of myself as unselfish. Everybody thinks of me, going to help the kids in Vietnam as heroic, and that makes me feel good.

"But my mom says I'm being selfish because I'm causing her and Dad to worry about me. Maybe she's right. Maybe I've been unwilling to risk the image I have of myself. If I let someone else really love me I might have to give up some of my independence and quit being so "heroic". It's probably the real reason that I've never married? If I did I'd just be an ordinary guy, like everybody else. Maybe I need to learn to be open to other's gifts and not always be the only giver."

Liesl did not pick up on Don's desire to help her in his response. She fell right back into her usual role of generic caregiver, grateful that he had taken the focus away from her. She was keeping him at arm's length, willing to help him but not to receive from him.

"Don, you can do both. Giving everything you've got to help others is just who you are. Someday you will be able to give to the wide world and have a family too, without changing who you are."

"Liesl, did you hear what you just said to me? What about you? Do you think you can do both, give constantly to generic "everyone" and also be able to receive someone totally? The words you just said to me, try saying them to yourself. You're not making sense."

Having her words turned on her was a complete shock to Liesl. As she looked up into Don's eyes he placed his hand on hers and her desire for him hit her with such might it was beyond her control. She stiffened, swallowed hard and teared. "Don, don't. I, I, I can't think about that now, while standing here with you. I'd better go." She turned away and started to pull away.

"Liesl, don't be afraid. We will not hurt each other, I promise." He clutched her hand more tightly, trying to turn her toward himself. She wanted so much to hold onto him, to fall into his arms and stay forever. But she couldn't allow herself to fall. She was too controlled. She was a nun. She tried to draw her hand from his.

"Don, I'll see you later." She tugged her hand loose and, without looking back into his eyes, which she knew would have been fatal for her, headed across the ship, picking up a book that she had laid on the bench.

"Liesl, just think about it. Give us a chance," he called after her. She sat facing away from him and opened her book. That the words were all wiggly, blurry lines didn't matter as she wasn't reading anyway. She just needed something to look at while she looked away from Don with all her strength.

Don stayed watching the water but like Liesl, he didn't really see anything. He didn't feel rejected; he only felt his longing for Liesl more intensely, the need to pursue her. But now he understood better how cautious he would have to be to get this right.

As he stood there with his mind and heart in that other world, he didn't notice Debra and Daiki approach and sit on the bench some distance behind him.

Chapter 11

DAIKI AND DEBRA

Debra and Daiki spoke to each other softly, shy about being heard, or even about being seen alone, together.

"Debra, when I saw you watching the sun rise at 5:00 this morning I couldn't disturb you. So, for about the fourth time, I went back downstairs instead. You are so beautiful when you're deep in meditation."

Debra smiled, so pleased that he liked her. "That kind of praise should embarrass me, Daiki, but coming from you it feels so good. Is this what love is like? I've never had anyone who is really good, love me except Barry and my parents, of course. Boyfriends have always been people who wanted to buy something from me with their affection."

Debra thought about her own words. "Maybe you just like that I meditate like you do. Others have said they love me because like them, I took drugs and could do drugs with them, or they liked me because of something else we had in common. You know that meditation makes everything and everyone seem beautiful and we have that in common." After a long pause Debra continued, "But I have so much to be forgiven for. I really need time to learn and to be sure I can do better."

"Debra, I'm trying to say more than just that I think you're beautiful. It's true, there is a way of seeing the beauty in everyone, but..." Daiki took Debra's hand. "I feel something more for you. I want to know you better." They looked deeply into each others' eyes.

"Deb, I have an idea. Can we have a real date? Let's do it tonight." Daiki snickered at his own idea. "I'll pick you up this evening at your door at 5:45 and take you to dinner. After dinner we can go for a walk together, come up here and look at the stars, maybe even fall in love."

Debra moved closer to Daiki and snuggled into him as he put his arm around her. "I'd love that. Let's do it." Then she ruined everything by being cautious:

"We better remember though, that our time is short. When you get off the ship at Yokohama, I have to go on with Barry. I have to do what I came to Japan for. Besides I can't leave Barry alone. He made this trip just to help me. You and I could keep in touch, though. Yokahama and Kobe are not so far apart."

They sat there together watching the water without speaking, each of them afraid of the next step. After a long, long minute, Daiki took Debra's chin in his free hand and brought it to his. He kissed her on the mouth first lightly, then firmly. Then they turned to each other, wrapping each other with their whole bodies. Daiki combed his hands through her hair. Their lips and tongues sensed one another's ears, eyelids and cheekbones. Daiki took Debra's hand and started to pull her toward the steps to take her to privacy but she ushered up all her strength and stopped him.

"No Daiki, we have to talk more first and I don't see how we can talk calmly right now in your cabin, with all these strong feelings that we both have. Tonight we'll talk to each other about ourselves on our date." They finally sat again, now so close they were like one.

Don suddenly became aware that he wasn't alone. He turned and saw Debra and Daiki together and felt the urge to rush over to Liesl and grab her, force himself on her. He felt so envious. For the first time he discovered that he really, really wanted a woman, this woman, in his life. Why could Daiki and Debra experience this happiness and he, why was he destined to reach for the unreachable star?

* * *

At 5:45, rather 5:43, Daki was at Debra's door. He was dressed in his black trousers and leather shoes, a white long-sleeved shirt with cuff links and wearing a black and yellow patterned tie. He knocked timidly. Debra had been waiting right at the door and opened it without pause. She was wearing a yellow silk dress with spaghetti straps and slim mid-thigh length skirt. Her sandy hair was pulled into a gentle pony tail with loose ends around her face. She wore brown two inch pumps. For a minute, they looked at each other with awe. Daiki reached out his arm and she took it. He had arranged with Goose to take Debra's seat for dinner so that she could take his and Debra and Daiki could sit together. The entire assembly was aware that this was first-date-night for this dashing couple.

The dinner tonight began with sushi and white wine. Salmon was the main course with a side of asparagus. When dessert was being served, Daiki and Debra excused themselves, anxious to proceed with their promenade. Hand in hand they walked each deck, ending on the bench under the stars. Debra had carried a soft beige wrap that they could snuggle with together if it was too cool. She threw it over their laps.

Daiki fumbled for words. "Debra, we've known each other for such a short time, but I'm so afraid to lose you if we go our separate ways after disembarking. I'm in love with you Debra. I think we could make a good life together.

"I know that you come from a very different culture from my own and there are many new things to learn about each other's families, and to adjust to. I've lived in America so I know a little about your country. I also know my traditional Japanese family might not like my choice...but Debra, that will change when they experience you. They will love you, I'm sure. I know that you are interested in Buddhism. Even if you choose not to become Buddhist, it wouldn't matter, because we both appreciate each other's spiritual life."

Debra started. "Daiki, I think I love you too, but there is so much we still don't know about each other. Are you aware that I've been a hard drug user? That's something one doesn't just get over in a year. And you're so perfect. You've worked so hard and been so clean. Can you be patient with my failings?"

Daiki was pleasantly relieved when Debra began sharing her weaknesses with him. Her willingness to be open, vulnerable with him meant to him that she was taking a giant step toward the intimacy with him that he was longing for.

"Debra, the steps you're taking to overcome your drug problem are more important to me than the drugs you took."

Encouraged to open-up further, Debra sank back into his body, her neck into the shoulder of the arm he had around her. She looked up into the millions of stars which created a sky that was more sparkly white than black. She could risk it now, knowing that he cared for her too. Better now than later. Debra wanted the man who would have her to have all of her. It was more than that. She didn't want some future revelation to demand an ugly forgiveness. She didn't want to have to beg for love despite who she was. The man she could be open to, could share her life with, would have to take her just as she is and still think of her as an equal.

"Daiki, I had a son last year. In fact, next week will be his second birthday."

Daiki was silent, then Debra felt his arm and chest stiffen. She didn't dare look into his face. Was this the moment when she would lose him?

Daiki, taken aback, swallowed and managed to come out with the words, "What did you do with him?" He asked it flatly, forcing his voice to hide his surprise. It wasn't a curiosity question. It was an accusing one, like he knew he wouldn't like her answer.

"I gave him up for adoption." She wanted to say much more but the useless words wouldn't come. She wanted to add that it was the best thing for him, that the child's father was also addicted, that she hadn't told Barry, that her parents would have been too angry to support her and the baby. She wanted to tell him that the adoptive parents allowed her to name the baby 'Barry'. She wanted to tell him her whole story, to help him understand and accept her decision, her life. Instead she was silent, tense. Unless he could listen without judging, an explanation was useless.

Daiki pulled away from her and walked over to the rail. He watched the white waters left behind by the ships forward thrust. "Left behind" felt very sad. Daiki felt very sad at the thought of leaving Debra behind but he could not go on with her. In one moment all had changed. What of the dishonor? His, hers, his fathers?

"Debra," he finally said, "I'm going to bed." He said it without looking at her, without expressing any emotion. "We can talk about this tomorrow."

Debra sat still, numb, for a long time, too chagrined at his reaction. Through all the difficulty endured and tears she shed while making the decision to give her son up for adoption, she never envisioned that it would cause the devastation she felt now, losing the man she wanted to love for a lifetime. Debra was crushed. How could she go on now? How could she face Daiki tomorrow to discuss his feelings? To tell him how she felt about his reaction? How could she face a final conversation, a final parting?

Chapter 12

PRICILLA'S BIRTHDAY

Goose couldn't hide his mischievousness. "Lily you go check under the bed while we watch out for you. If there are more bottles, she's getting it from the captain. If there are fewer bottles, she's giving it to the captain."

"Goose, I told you not to tell anyone. Now you've gone and said it in front of everyone."

"Lily all the people here, you've already told."

"Oh dear, I am such a blabbermouth? Okay, I'll go look for you."

Lillian tiptoed into her room. She was gone a minute, opened her door slowly, peeked out, walked stealthily around the lounge and plopped down in a chair. "I'll be! There's a whole case there now. Her laughter burst through the fingers covering her mouth. "That means that after she puts her shoes under his bed and they have their cocktail hour together, she comes back here with a bottle in that big purse."

Allie broke in. "Not to change the subject, but tomorrow is my mom's seventieth birthday. Will you help me celebrate it?"

Goose raked back the hair above his ears with his fingers as he always did when he was excited. "Ooh, this'll be fun. The girls can make some cards for each of us to say "Happy Birthday." And we've gotta have a birthday cake. Who knows how to bake?"

"You've got to be kidding. How can we bake on this ship?"Allie asked.

"You sell me short," Goose said. "Don't you know that I was a sailor for years. I know everything about how to do whatever we need to do on a ship. We'll do it tonight after most of the crew is gone to bed. It will give us something to do on our twenty-fifth hour today. Allie, you stay with your mom so she won't know what we're doing. The rest of us meet here at 11:00 tonight and we'll break into the kitchen. Who wants to decorate the lounge tonight?"

"I'll stay back here and work on decorations," Ethel said. If anybody has anything, bright colored, shirts, wrapping paper, confetti or anything to contribute that I can hang around to serve as a decoration, drop it off in my room before you go to the kitchen."

"I'm going to talk to Beverly about her stash. Surely she'll be willing to contribute something to Priscilla's seventieth birthday," this contribution from Lillian.

At dinner that evening the atmosphere was gay, belying the unsettled feelings of Debra, Daiki, Liesl and Don. Barry's short wave radio had not yet started to pick up radio waves. The time was getting long for some of the passengers while it was too short for love birds trying to settle their feelings. When they returned from dinner, Lillian grabbed Goose's arm, winked at him and followed Beverly to their room.

"Bev, we really need your help," she began. Tomorrow is Priscilla's seventieth birthday and we need to celebrate royally. Think you could toss in, ahem, some spirits, to make the occasion grand?"

It took Beverly a minute to react. "Lillian, everyone has a birthday every year. What's the big deal?" Her chest felt tight, then her shoulder and arm muscles tightened. She flopped down on the side of the bed. "They all know, don't they? They are going to embarrass me into admitting it openly?

"Lillian, if I say 'no' you'll think I'm selfish and if I say 'yes' you'll say I'm a whore. It's better if I don't participate. You and your friends can have a good time and have me to talk about if I'm not there."

"Oh Beverly, I'm so sorry you feel this way and wouldn't enjoy the party. I wish I knew why you have such a solid wall built around yourself. I wish I could help you. This party will be one we'll always remember."

"Priscilla won't remember." Beverly got up, reached under the head of the bed and brought out a bottle of Bailey's Irish Creme that had never been opened and reached it to Lillian. "If you take this I'll be too embarrassed to come to the party. Its me or the booze, not both."

"Well then, Bev, it'll be you." Lillian did not take the bottle so Beverly dropped her arm. "We will just have to do without the booze. We want you to be there." Lillian said as she turned and left the room to see what she could do to help with the party. She didn't want to give Beverly another chance to refuse to join them tomorrow.

Beverly lay down on the bed and stared at the ceiling. Of all things, why should I care, she thought. But when Lillian walked out, Beverly realized, my heart started beating like Elvis's drummer. I was almost in panic, she thought. I've never believed in introspection but here I am "introspecting." When Lillian walked out a minute ago, I wanted desperately to call her back. But I was afraid that I'd let down my wall, as she called it. Wall? They say I have a wall, but if this is an example, my wall is almost like a tissue paper divider.

* * *

At 11:00 P.M. they were all gathered in the lounge except Priscilla. Allie said that her mother was sleeping.

"If you want to go with the others, its okay. If Priscilla gets up and comes out looking for you, I'll take care of it," Ethel encouraged Allie.

"I'm not going to the kitchen," Beverly announced.

"Good. Then you can stay here and help me with the decorations if you will," Ethel said. They all left for the kitchen leaving Ethel and Beverly alone in the lounge.

"Beverly, look at how Goose and Allie are enjoying each other," Ethel said. "I'm so happy for them."

"Well, I'm not. They're both old enough to have more sense. A person can lead a worthwhile life without having to have a man. Allie's mother needs her. And Goose, what does she see in him?" Beverly looked glum, her eyes glancing back and forth as she sought for more accusations she could make. "And Debra, flirting with the Japanese guy. What do you suppose those two do up there on the top deck at five in the morning?" After a pause she added, "and Ethel, let me tell you something. That Liesl of yours is no saint either. Have you noticed how she looks at Don with those twinkling eyes? What kind of respect can I have for her?"

She had hit the nerve of Ethel's fear. "Look Beverly, I think I better work alone. If we keep gabbing we won't get done before the others get back."

Beverly gladly went to her room while Ethel proceeded to climb on chairs and hang all the bright colors she had received, a pair of jockey shorts with dinosaurs on them from Goose, a yellow blouse from Debra, a red sweater from Allie and a big 'Happy Birthday' sign made by Debra and Liesl using sheets of cardboard that Captain Mack had found for them in the food pantry. When she finished she sat in an easy chair in the lounge waiting for the others' return. Then Ethel fell into a sound sleep.

Goose led the way to the kitchen where the cooking was done before being placed on dumb waiters for delivery to the passengers' dining room. He cautioned all to be quiet as they were in the crew's quarters and might be heard. Every click or bang of a dish or a pan brought giggles, and when Don spilled half of the cake batter while carrying it to the oven they laughed so hard that Liesl and Debra had to sit on the floor to hold their stomachs while they tried to keep their laughter quiet.

Then they debated on whether to scoop up and use the batter or start over with a new mixture. They chose the latter which added another half hour to their venture. When all was finished Goose directed them to return to their quarters.

"I'll stay here to take the cake from the oven when its done. Lillian, you take the icing upstairs with you. We can ice the cake tomorrow." They all returned, each to their own room. Liesl woke Ethel in the lounge and told her what a great job she had done with the decorations. Then they went to their room. A minute later, Allie knocked on their door.

"Where's my mom?" she asked Ethel, confused.

"She's not in your room?"

Allie was frantic. "No, you didn't see her leave?

"Allie, go and get Goose. He'll know what to do, Ethel said. I'll get all the others from their rooms and have them start to search. She's probably in the wrong room or bathroom. She can't have gone far." Ethel and Liesl started knocking on each door to search and alert all the passengers.

"Beverly isn't here either," Lillian said. "Maybe she took Priscilla for a walk or something." They divided up the search team. Goose and Allie returned with the cake and placed it in Lillian's room. Priscilla had not followed them. After about a half hour of search most of them had returned to the lounge. No Priscilla, no Beverly.

"The right thing would be to hit the alarm in the dining room," Goose said, "But since Beverly's missing too, I think we should check with Captain Mack first. If Bev is with him, she may know where Priscilla is and we wouldn't have to wake the whole ship. It's my responsibility to do that since I took us on the "wild Goose chase" to bake a cake. I'll be right back. Ethel, please stay with Allie, I know she's panic stricken." Goose left.

Allie was shaking, afraid that her knees wouldn't hold her up, but she wouldn't stay in the lounge. "What if she's out on the deck?

She could fall overboard? Oh my God, what if she has fallen overboard? We'd never know what happened." Each person said something to assure Allie that this couldn't have happened yet all knew that it could.

Goose returned with Captain Mack. Neither of them had seen Priscilla or Beverly. It was time for Captain Mack to turn on the alarm. Maybe Priscilla had gotten into the crews' quarters and would be found there. Captain Mack would notify the pilot to shut down the forward thrust but not to turn around.

Ethel quickly took down the decorations from the lounge, except for the 'Happy Birthday' sign. This was no time to be silly with Allie distressed, bewildered, devastated and two of their friends lost.

The rest of the night passed with the crew searching their quarters and lighting all the decks and passageways. Allie walked the decks round and round until, about six o'clock, when Goose insisted she lie down. She had been searching the decks since one A.M. If she became any more exhausted she might slip and fall overboard herself. He sat at her bedside to keep her there while she restlessly, tried to sleep, jumping up with every sound. It was strange that Beverly was also missing. It wasn't like her to get lost on ship.

At 0600 the second engineer descended to the boiler room to check the dials, temperature, power thrust. The ship must proceed regardless of the grief on board. It was impossible to search the waters, not knowing if or when someone had been lost, any number of hours ago in that vastness. If that had happened they couldn't be alive anymore anyway with no safety jackets or life boat. Buried at sea on her seventieth birthday, no one could say the words everyone was thinking.

At 0602, Engineer Columbo heard his second engineer calling an SOS on his pager. "Boiler room, Boiler room. SOS boiler room." He grabbed ahold of two other crew members and headed immediately to the boiler room. There they found the two women. Priscilla was lying with one foot caught between pipes carrying steam from the boiler. Her foot was severely burned by the hot pipe, but probably could be saved because of the robe that Beverly had managed to force between her foot and the pipes. When he found them, Beverly was sitting on the cold cement floor cradling Priscilla's head. The engineer needed the help of his crew mates to loosen Priscilla's foot without anyone else being burned and hopefully, without any other serious injury to her leg.

Wheelchairs were brought down for both women who were delivered sweat soaked, and exhausted to the lounge. Captain Mack had informed first Alexis, then the others, that the women were found and not seriously injured. All waited for them with a sense of foreboding. To Captain Mack "not seriously injured" may mean "alive." and nothing more.

When Allie saw her mom she ran to her, sobbing, barely able to catch her breath. Goose went to Beverly and hugged her long and tight mindless of her sweaty odor, soaked clothes and matted hair.

Both women were put to bed posthaste to await the medic to treat the burn on Priscilla's leg and check Beverly. The medic was empowered to administer oral antibiotics and light analgesics in emergency and so, was able to start treatment for Priscilla. Then Alexis, Priscilla and Beverly slept. Right through lunch time they slept while the others planned.

"I can't wait to hear what happened to them," Ethel said. "I feel so responsible."

"I know all I need to know," Goose said. "What I know is that you, Ethel, are not to blame for falling asleep. I would have done the same thing if I had to sit here and wait while all the rest of us were having a good time.

And most important, I know that Beverly is my hero. If it weren't for Bev's escapades with Mack, we probably would have lost Priscilla or at best, she would be losing her leg. Beverly must have been going to visit Mack when she found Priscilla. Why else would she be roaming the ship at midnight?"

"I think we should do something special for Beverly" Don said. "She'll never suspect that a party is planned for her as well as Priscilla."

Debra wanted to know, "Is the party back on?"

Liesl was adamant. "You bet it is. We better have it after dinner though, instead of after lunch, so Priscilla and Allie and Beverly can sleep as long as they need to."

"I'll redecorate, so everyone please give me back, all the stuff you gave me before that I returned to you," Ethel agreed.

Daiki had an idea. "If I help you Ethel, we can decorate during dinner time so it will be a surprise for Priscilla and Beverly when they come back from dinner. Deb, maybe you and Liesl could make a few more cards like you did for Priscilla. They could say thank you to Beverly."

The ladies did get up for dinner. They didn't seem to notice that Ethel and Daiki were missing from their tables in the dining room they were so wrapped in their stories. When all were finished eating, they had been told 'no dessert tonight,' and they had turned their clocks back from 1900 to 1800, they returned to the lounge.

Big signs hung side by side said "Happy Seventieth Birthday Priscilla" and "Thank You Beverly". The whole group burst out in song when they opened the door, led by Debra and played on her guitar by Liesl: "For She's a Jolly Good Fellow," "Happy Birthday," then "I Want a Girl, Just Like the Girl that Married Dear Old Dad." During the third song Beverly grabbed Goose's arm and pulled him over to her room, closing the door behind them.

When the song was finished she opened her door and Goose exited carrying a whole case of bottles of alcohol.

As they were laughing, Debra started the last song over again with the words changed to "I want a drink, just like the drink that pickled my old man." The chocolate cake with raspberry preserve filling and white icing was the best ever despite being lopsided, actually totally collapsed on one side, and made with illicit ingredients. Captain Mack arrived carrying his contribution, a gallon of ice cream.

"I'll have a word with you, Mr. Ash," Mack said when he saw the cake. "After the festivities are over, of course."

Goose's laugh sounded like the hooting ship. "Now Mack, you can't imagine that I had anything to do with that cake, purty as it is. Why, I'm just a passenger on this ship and we hain't got no means for baking. We men, just 'ordered out' for Pricilla's birthday. You must agree that we had to celebrate this somehow."

"Do the honorees have anything to say?" Lillian asked.

Beverly, for the first time it seemed to the others, was light-hearted and for the first time looked relaxed with her mates. She hadn't had time to fix her pompadour so her blond hair hung limp, like a natural pageboy. To everyone's surprise, she wore jeans, that they wouldn't have guessed she owned, and a big oversized, white sweat shirt. And most of all, unlike her usual critical statements, she wanted to contribute to the camaraderie. "Yes, I have to speak," she said. Then, mustering up the courage to address them all she said, "I can't believe the lengths that Priscilla will go to, in order to have a memorable birthday." She said it most affectionately and winked at Priscilla, while they all hooted, laughed and clapped. Then she added, "I am dumbfounded that you all included me in this party." Her voice wavered, showing her seldom seen emotion. "I don't deserve you. All I can offer..." she giggled through her trembling..."is a little booze," and then she broke into a hearty laugh, joining in the fun.

Alexis wanted to help her mom contribute but didn't know if she was up to it. "Mom, do you want to say anything?"

Priscilla was up to it. "Yes, all I can say is..." Then she started to laugh and couldn't stop herself. Priscilla laughed as she hadn't for a long time. Her leg, wrapped with a bulky dressing and propped up on another chair, she forgot for a moment, the pain in her leg. Her stomach hurt with laughter more than her burnt leg hurt, because she was laughing so hard. One after another they all started laughing. They didn't yet know what was so funny, what Priscilla would come out with. They just laughed at her laughter. "All I can say is, and she broke up again. "All I can say is that..." the room was filled with hilarious laughter as she finally got it out. "It looks like neither God nor the devil wants me."

Even God and the devil must have been laughing.

Chapter 13

BEVERLY

It was a sunny morning with calm waters and only the small breeze created by the movement of the ship. Beverly found an empty lounging chair on the fore of their main deck. She was not in the mood for conversation when Lillian approached her. She had a lot to think about. Her own family was disinterested in her and she was going to gradually lose the people that were like a new family for her, as they, one-by-one alighted from this ship.

"May I join you, Bev?" Lillian didn't wait for an answer, just sat down next to Beverly. "Do you feel like telling me what happened yesterday, to you and Priscilla?"

"I guess so," Beverly reluctantly began. "You were all gone to the kitchen. I saw Ethel sleeping in the lounge so I peeked in Priscilla's room to be sure that she was okay, and saw that she was gone. I figured Allie must have come for her and brought her downstairs to the kitchen, so it would be a good time for me to go...you know, for a walk someplace. I stopped by the kitchen first and saw you all in there having such a good time. I figured you wouldn't like it if I interrupted, but I kept looking and, still didn't see Priscilla. I got worried. I started walking around looking for her in all the usual places. No Priscilla.

"I didn't want to frighten everyone so I just started looking for her myself. When I got to the second level, I realized there was more noise than usual coming from the basement level so I creeped down the stairs and was surprised to see the boiler room door open. The crew never leaves that open because its so hot and noisy in there. So, I went down to see what was going on and there was Priscilla lying on the floor with her foot between two pipes. I don't know how she fell. I tried for a while to pry her foot loose but I was hurting her and I was afraid I'd break something or pull it out of socket. I didn't know if she might have broken a hip or something. I told her to holler loud as she could.

"We both hollered for a few minutes but nobody heard us and I realized that I was just making her more anxious by telling her to holler. I was afraid what she would do if I left her to go for help, so I sat down on the floor and put her head in my lap. I kept saying 'just rest, Priscilla, someone will be here soon. Just rest. Just rest.' She would doze off, then the boiler would turn over and frighten her awake and she'd cry a little.

"Then after, it seemed like forever, I heard the sound of someone at the other end of the boiler room so I held tight to her head and screamed as loud as I could and the engineer heard me. He rushed over and saw us, then called for help and rescued us."

"Oh dear, Beverly, you were so brave. You are a very kind person."

"Do you think so Lillian?"

"I know so. You don't seem to know it though, Beverly, I wonder why you can't relax with us, why you won't let yourself be loved? Do you have family, Bev?"

"Sure. I came to America to visit my two kids. Alma lives in Rhode Island. I flew there first. I didn't warn them I was coming because I didn't want to give them a chance to say they didn't have time for me. So they said it when I got there. Alma called Albert in San Francisco to see if she could just send me there. He said I could visit but not for long because he was busy too. So I saw as much of the country as I had the energy for. I looked around Washington D.C., I saw the buildings and millions of people and Marshall Fields in Chicago, I saw the mountains from downtown Denver and I spent a few days seeing San Francisco before I called Albert. Then after two days with Albert I decided, why should I hurry to go home? I might as well see the world on the way. So I made a reservation for this ship."

"Beverly, it must be very lonely for you. Maybe you can find a way to fill in some of the spaces in your life. It would be good for your children too, to see the good things you are doing of your life instead of them just thinking of you as a burden. It might even help them to understand you better. Maybe someday they'd let you back into their lives ."

"But what can I do, Lillian? How can I 'fill the spaces'?"

"I'm going to help you think about it. We'll both think about it and talk some more. What kind of things do you enjoy? Besides men, I mean."

"Lily, I don't always..."

"I know, Bev, I was just teasing you. I shouldn't have said that. You are fine with me whatever you do with your time. You are a good person, Bev. Just remember that." Lillian got up from her seat, gave Beverly a kiss on the cheek and squeezed her hand before turning to leave. "I'm going to leave you alone now to think about that. I know that together, we can come up with the dream plan for you."

Beverly squeezed her hand back, then jumped up to hug Lillian. "Thank you, Lillian," she whispered. "Maybe you can help me. I don't know where to start, but I will try if you can help me."

Chapter 14

BECKONING

Liesl didn't usually lay down in the middle of the day, but she needed to be alone to think. There was no space on this ship. Wherever she went, there was somebody, trying to be kind or not so kind, it didn't matter. Alone is what she needed. It seemed to Liesl that her course was being plotted by someone else. She felt destined, pulled, beckoned. She needed to convince herself that she was thinking straight, not doing anything rash. She needed to make her own decision about her own life. The person she really wanted to discuss things with was Don, but that was perilous. Their feelings were too strong for them to think rationally together.

Then, of course, the minute she lay down, here was Ethel entering her space again. "Liesl, we have to talk. I'm becoming concerned about you. Others too, have noticed," Ethel began.

"And what are you so concerned about Ethel?"

"Your vocation, Liesl. Getting too close to the men on this ship could be dangerous for your vocation. In just about two weeks we'll be off the ship and our lives can go on as they always have, committed to God and his people. Don't put that in jeopardy."

Liesl sat up on the bed and drew her knees up with her arms. This is what she had been trying to have time to think about, alone. The perspective that Ethel offered pushed her leaning tower a little further over. Avoiding "Go on as it always has," was the reason Liesl was on this ship, the reason she had fought her way out of previous assignments.

"Ethel, I started this journey so committed to it's purpose, God and the poor, and my participation in that love affair of His. I still am committed to it, but some of the people on his ship are opening my mind to other possibilities, other ways to accomplish my purpose."

"What could you possibly find that would be better than what you are now doing?" asked Ethel.

"When I saw how Beverly, an ordinary woman, in fact, one that most of us didn't think much of, risked her reputation and maybe even her life for Priscilla who has dementia," Liesl paused, looked at the ceiling and mused, "and hearing Barry and Debra's story, how he has risked his career because he loves her..."

"Liesl, you have your own mission."

"Yes Ethel, I do. Maybe it's not the same as yours though. Maybe its not too late for me to start on a new venture."

"Liesl, don't you consider Thailand a new venture? Isn't this adventure enough for you?"

"Of course, it is if its right for me, Ethel, but I'm feeling the need to, not only help others, but to open myself up more to others' gifts to me.

I don't expect you to understand this, and that's why I need to ponder it myself, without all of your caution. It seems to me that my desire to create and nurture life wherever I can, is God's call at this time in my life. It may now be my new vocation.

"God has been here as Beverly finding Priscilla and as Barry saving Debra from her mistakes. He's here as Goose and Allie and you and me. He's here as us when we help each other or make each other laugh. He doesn't need us to be nuns to do this. He just needs us to be open and available. I think He wants from us, whatever we want to give Him, and that may change as our lives change."

"I can't believe what I'm hearing you say, Liesl. If you think you can live two lives, flirt with these men, then come and be a heroine to the people in Thailand with Leprosy...Liesl, I think you need counseling. As soon as we get off this ship I'll call Father Dole.

He'll probably call you back to the U.S. for a retreat. You need God's forgiveness, not mine."

"Ethel, I hoped I could help you to understand this, but if not, you'll just have to accept my decision. Whatever I decide, it's not a rash decision. For years I've been struggling with the meaning of the community in my life. God being the priority in my life has not changed since I was fifteen. But I've been exposed over the years, to more ways of living that out. When I was younger, religious life seemed like the only way a person could belong to God. Now I see the world differently, maybe more completely. Now it seems that creating harmony for myself, those around me and the world, is the way I show my gratitude to Him for my life and their lives. My experience of the people on this ship is confirming this belief for me.

Liesl continued, "I'm not asking forgiveness, I think courage and insight, not forgiveness, are what I need. I need time to think about what is right for me, and I can't do that with your contribution, because you are coming from the same place as my childhood experience that brought me to the convent in the first place.

"I am concerned though, about leaving you alone in Thailand. If I decide I need a leave of absence I could work with you in Thailand as a lay person until the Community can send you a replacement," Liesl said.

"No way would I let you do that. I will have plenty of help, Ethel answered. "I couldn't watch you every day, living as though you had no vocation. Father Dole will send someone else who would be more faithful, if you're not there. I wouldn't be alone."

Ethel obviously wasn't able to process what she saw as Liesl's change in thinking, in commitment. Liesl stood and gave Ethel an unreturned hug, then left the room as fast as she could walk slowly. Her thoughts were out in the open now. A new life was beckoning.

Chapter 15

RESCUE

"What are you so glum about little lady?" Goose had watched Debra go from animated to dull since her big date with Daiki.

"Oh Goose, I'm so sad."

Goose took Debra's arm and sat her down at his side on the top deck. "Can you tell me about it, Debra?"

After a few sniffles she blurted it out. "Daiki is the kindest man I've ever known, but he can't handle the whole of me. If he can't, probably no one can."

"What can't he handle, Debra?"

Debra was relieved to blurt out the reason for her heartbreak. "I think he knew, everybody knows that I'm an addict. I didn't think I'd ever have the strength to stay clean, but its been a whole year now. I'm searching for strength to stay off drugs and I'm doing it. I think maybe Buddhism will help me. That's why Barry and I are on this trip, so I can search out and live Buddhism for a while in Asia, where it's a way of life.

Now I've met Daiki. He said he thinks I'm strong and compassionate already. I thought I just needed to tell him the whole truth about me. I guess telling the whole truth doesn't work if it's my truth. Goose, Barry doesn't even know. I've had a child that I gave up for adoption. When I told Daiki, he really freaked out. He couldn't even talk about it. How can I face him the rest of this trip? How can I say goodbye to him? How can I tell a monk my story? How can I keep trying to meditate when I'm such a phony?'

After Goose let her cry in his arms for awhile he took her two shoulders in his big hands and stood her up facing him. "Now you listen to me Debra. You hain't just beautiful like other ladies, you've known. You're beautiful through and through. Look how you put a song in us at Priscilla's party. Look how Barry struts like a peacock when he watches you, you do him so proud. And the most you've done is what you've done for Daiki. You made him relax and be lighthearted maybe for the first time in his life. He needs you for that. You show him to love real life, not just book life. Spose no one ever loved him just for himself, apart from praising how smart he is."

Debra was flustered, unsettled. He could tell it in her restless eyes.

"You make him listen to you, Debra."

"Do you think I can?" She was frightened of the thought of confrontation; sure she'd be on the losing side.

"Course you can. You can help him better than anybody." He wiped the tears from her face and replaced them with a big wet smack. "Now you go on and figure out what you're going to say to Daiki."

Chapter 16

BACKBONE

The clouds had diminished the strength of the sunshine but the wind had not yet picked up. They were seated on the fourth deck aft. That had become the passengers' talking place, kind of like a psychiatrist's couch or a beautician's salon or a bartenter's bar. Daiki was properly groomed as always, Goose was in Khaki shorts and forest green tee and white socks with his leather sandals. In only four more days they would reach their first port, Yokohama, Japan where Daiki was scheduled to alight. Time was short.

"Daiki, I have something important to say to you," Goose said. "What has happened to your beautiful Debra? She's walking around here with that morose look on her face ever since your first and only date. Tain't like her. What did you do to her?"

"Goose, before that night I thought I was in love with Debra. I knew about the drugs she took but she's overcoming her addiction. I thought she was so perfect for me and that I could help her, too. Then I discovered that she has too much past. She's been in more trouble than I ever guessed.

"How can I take her to my home? My father will say she is unworthy of him and his father. I will feel self-disgust whether for telling him I accept her or for hiding the truth. My mom will cry if I stand up to my father. There will be no dowry, no grandchildren in their village if they don't choose the bride." Daiki closed down the subject. It was over for him. His choice was made.

Goose was not about to let that happen.

"You are not ashamed of her. I know better. You're afraid. Afraid of what your parents will think, afraid of disinheritance. You're afraid of your father's anger. Don't give me that 'Japanese culture' line. You're not ashamed, you're afraid. And it's not your father's fault that she won't be accepted, it's yours.

"You have to decide: Do you want to be timid or confident? Do you want to be angry at Debra for her past mistakes or angry at your parents for being narrow minded or angry at yourself for being a jerk? Do you want to be proud that love made you stand up and be strong or sorry and lonely the rest of your life because it didn't?"

They were silent for awhile but Goose wasn't finished.

"You should be proud that Debra did a good thing for her babe. You should be proud that she trusted you enough to tell you about him. Telling your parents or not telling them about her past won't matter once you decide you're proud of her and everything about her. You can be proud she birthed her young'un and saw to it havin a good life. You and she will decide together how to face other people. You got lots of things to decide together. That's just one of 'em. You will decide where to live, where to work and how to raise your young 'uns if you're blessed with some. Daiki, you don't have to decide now about marriage, only decide if you can open up to Debra, let her into your life, stick up for her."

Daiki knew Goose was right but his mind flitted through all the possible scenarios at home. How would he introduce Debra? Getting off the ship with a woman by the hand wouldn't allow for gradual introduction. His parents would immediately know that he was thinking of marriage to her, before he could make excuses for having her with him.

"Daiki, you are the first son in your family. You may have to be the one to lead the flock, you know, like the goose that flies first. You are the first son, the one who will make it easier for your brothers and sisters to find their own way in the world. You may have to soften up your parents, not because you want to rebel, but because you need to stand up for what you believe in and love. Maybe that's why they sent you to America een though they didn't know it."

"Goose, I think I'm...what do you Americans say, the chicken, not the goose." Daiki snickered at himself. "Do chickens have, how do you say, backbones?"

"Daiki, are you going to let Debra have more backbone than you ? She has the guts to face rejection from everybody and you don't even have enough guts to face your paw? Maybe she can help you. She has experience with this. Lots of folks have told her she was wrong before now. They told her she couldn't beat her troubles, but she proved they were wrong. Do you want her to be wrong about you?" Daiki's thoughts rumbled around in his head like bowling balls that got loose in an alley. Goose could almost see and hear the thoughts in Daiki's head.

"Goose, I know you are right. I have only four days to get ready to meet my parents, but maybe I can do something about the mess I made. First I must see if Debra will forgive me.

When I am with Debra I like myself better. She sees me, not my education or nationality. She doesn't say I'm stoic, she says I'm thoughtful. She doesn't say I'm smart, she says I have insight. With Debra I appreciate the wind on my face and quiet time, especially when we're just sitting there doing nothing. The time I waste with her is as important as my work."

Goose sighed. "Ah, yes, the fox friend of Antoine De Saint Exupery's Little Prince: 'It is the time you have wasted for your friend, that makes him so important. I couldn't have said it better. " Daiki, go waste some time with Debra."

Chapter 17

RECASTING

As he approached Alexis sitting alone at the table in the lounge, Goose could see that her head was down, her shoulders quaking. He walked over to her to sit down at her side. Putting one arm around her shoulders, he took her chin in his other brawny hand until her tears ran down his hand. Then her tears turned into trembling sobs.

"My bonnie girl, Allie, what could be vexing you so much to make you shake like a wet dog?" he asked, not knowing whether to tease her or to be sad with her at this moment.

Her few words, hyphenated by jerks, told the whole story. "Goose, I'm afraid I might be falling in love with you," she cried.

"Well now, is that so bad to make you cry like this?" He asked. "I'm kind of taken with you too. I know I'd get the better end of the stick if we was to fall in love, but I'd try to see it weren't too bad for you"

"Goose, you know that's not true," she smiled at him even in her distress, then broke into a louder cry. "I'm so afraid of losing you?" Allie continued to shake until she could get the words out. "How could I ask you to come with me? I hate that condo I live in. It would be too small for us. It's all wrong. Its walls close in if I paint them strong colors and if they're light the place is blah. It's too hot or too cold. It's too bare if I leave it empty and it's too cluttered if I decorate it. It's, It's..." She banged her fist on the table, then tore and crunched the magazine sheets lying there and made a circle of them on the table. She pointed into the circle. "Could you live in a little place like that?"

Goose grabbed her powerfully. He didn't say another word, but knew exactly what it was she hated so much. It wasn't the condo. She hated being alone in it again. She hated the thought of watching, while her mother, who might have to come and live with her, would slowly deteriorate. She hated sharing her space and her life with the painful knowledge, that when her mother was gone, her purpose in life would be gone. She even hated Goose. Finding Goose might only mean she would have to lose him again.

Reaching age thirty without a fiancee, Allie had watched her friends one after another, pair up, break up the old gang. Each time she felt more lonely until the day she was feeling rock bottom. That was the day her friend Julie told her of the good fortune in her life, as she held up her left hand to show off the rock on her ring finger.

It also was the day Allie chose to embrace her fate. She was tired of looking at every man as a potential date. She would let her work absorb her time. It could provide her with friendship and support her ego.

That was the day she decided to buy a condo. No point in waiting any longer to own her own place. She might as well face the fact that she would always be alone. She searched and searched the area. St. Luis Obispo was a beautiful town with country estates and little houses on acres of oceanside property, but after looking at all that beauty, Allie chose a small condo. I'm always at work or at school, why pay for extra space with patios and gardens to take care of? It's just me living there, she decided. I'll get a window box and plant a few geraniums. That's enough of an idyll for me.

Her working days had been a good time for her. She couldn't wait to get to work in the morning. She was important there. Anyway, there was no one waiting for her at home. At work a lot of people looked up to her. She was creating a material that wouldn't disintegrate on the moon. It was to be used for the flag that would be placed on the moon when the Apollo mission, Columbia landed there. Who else but her and her team had ever done that? And she designed air pressure suits for the astronauts, another first. Their lives depended somewhat on her.

"Goose, if I'm away from work for just one year, the young scientists will pass me by. The top rung of my career ladder is just the first rung of theirs and I'm not ready to lose my job, my work."

"Yes," Goose agreed, "I'm just the opposite of you, always been on the move. At first I was fretful. I needed to run off. I was just a colt myself. Pretendin to be a Paw to them girls was just too much burden for me. Soon I found that the sea, with constant move to new jobs, in new places, with new faces was steadyin for me, not just an escape. What could be better than weeks on the ocean waves. I was proud to be at sea. I became a happy wanderer. The sea was where I could restore my wits and feel like I was at home.

"Allie, I don't want no girl in every port now. You are all of them. Heck, you're like a port itself for me."

"But Goose, what if you got restless again? I couldn't ask you to sit and wait for me to come home from work every day."

"And Allie, I couldn't ask you to wait at home for me while I wandered. And I couldn't ask you to leave your job and go with me, lessen you wanted to."

"Goose, I don't know how to explain what you've done for me; it's hard to tell you what its like to not be sad. Have you ever squinted for a long time with the bright sun in your eyes? Then you put on a pair of sunglasses and your whole face relaxes. You can feel not squinting." Goose nodded his agreement.

"Or if you've had a terrible pain, then finally fall asleep. When you wake up in the morning, the pain is gone. You can actually feel not having pain. That's what it feels like having you in my life. I can actually feel not being sad and alone."

"Princess, you do me too much honor," he said almost shyly, "but tell me about why you've been so sad."

"I think my sadness started when my dad died and it's been with me all of my life. Oh, I was happy when my mom or brother visited, when I was successful at work or received honors in school, but beneath all that, I've always been haunted by emptiness at the end of the day. My dad, he was my whole life when I was a child until he died suddenly in that mine. Everyone in town was heavyhearted that year. I was only ten years old. I didn't feel I could burden my mom or anyone else with my tears, so I kept my grief to myself.

Then I thought I had to take it upon myself to fix things for my mom. Leaving West Virginia for college in California was the hardest thing I've ever done. I felt so guilty about leaving her alone. Even though, first my school and then my work, were across the country, I kept constant contact with her and kept her as my closest friend. I traveled to be with her often and never had my own family to take her place. "Now I've met you and...what if I'm falling in love?" With that, Allie broke into loud uncontrollable sobs.

After a hug so tight it almost hurt, the sobs became sniffles and she could speak again. "My whole life would change if I followed you or if you came with me. How could I take care of Mom and be with you? And what about my job? If I gave up my job to travel with you, I could never find another job like the one I have now."

"Heck Allie, We need to think of one problem at a time not all of 'em at once. I know we can fix 'em all if we really want to.

"Now about your mom, I'd help with Priscilla if she'd have me. Anyway she likes me better 'n you. She likes having a man's arms around her. We'd have to live in a bigger house though, the three of us, lessen she stays in Germany like she says she might.

"Now the job, that's another thing. I haint never had a woman support me. I'd have to give up some of my loneliness and live in that St.Luis Obispo place. Long as you'd let me take ol' Priscilla over to the seashore while you're at work, I'd put up with it. I'll muse on that problem Allie, but I'd be so proud of you workin on them space ships, I jus don't know how I'd get too restless. Every day when you come home, you'd make me feel like we're makin it so's someday other people, maybe even our grandkids, can fly to the moon.

"Now, that 'woman in every port,' that's just talkin fer fun. I know you'd make up for my woman in every port, heck, you already do and we haint never even had sex together," he said.

"Allie, can I kiss you? We might as well start being familiar." Goose didn't wait for an answer. He leaned down and kissed her long but gently on the lips. Then he took her head in his two hands and kissed her again. Then he looked so lovingly into her eyes that all her fears vanished. Suddenly she knew he would be there for her through better or worse. He held her tight. She already felt like one with him.

"I guess I should ask ol' Priscilla for permission to court you," he said while still holding her. "It'll make it feel more official."

Allie snickered. "Ol' Priscilla will love the idea."

* * *

Priscilla, shifted around in her chair in the lounge while Goose adjusted her elevated foot on its cushion. "I've always loved Alexis best Goose," Priscilla said, "but there were times. Although she was younger than her brothers, she always wanted to do them one better. She was better than them in school and better than them in making friends. I wanted each of them to be best at something. It's hard to remember most of the things I should tell you, but I do remember one time I was so mad at her. Ricky loved skipping stones on the lake by Ma and Pa's house. He practiced and practiced. Then the first time she tried, her stone skipped more times and further than his. "Goose, do you think you can put up with her being better than you all the time?"

"Heck, them young sailors are already better than me. Anyhows, she'll never be a better sailor than me. I'll have one thing on her."

"Don't you count on it Goose. Now another thing, this is the most important thing, you asked if I could do without her? Even though I've always been her priority because she was single, we've lived far away from each other all these years. I didn't need her baby-sitting me then and I don't need her to do it now. It's Allie's turn to have her sailor just like I had my miner. Besides, I don't want her hovering over me watching me get helpless. I'd rather have someone do that who won't be so hurt by it.

"Anyway, Allie said I might get to stay in Germany with Eddie and my grandchildren. Wouldn't that be wonderful?"

"Well then, Priscilla, I have your permission to court Allie?"

" Aah Goose, not only my permission, but oh heck, my blessing too." Priscilla felt that even her own dreams were coming true.

Chapter 18

HOPE

Daiki knocked on Debra's door, his mind overflowing with ways to say "I'm sorry" and fears that she would close the door before he could get the words out. When she came to the door ten thousand minutes later, his voice wouldn't emit a single sound. His eyes searched the floor and her bare feet, then tears welled up then ran down his face. Debra reached for his chin with both hands and brought his face to hers, lightly kissing his lips.

They made love to each other for what seemed like a long time, standing in the doorway, fully clothed, eyes locked and longing. Then Debra said, "Daiki, please find Barry and ask him to give us some time alone in our room. We need to talk without interruption."

When Daiki returned to the room Debra was sitting up, still dressed in jeans and grey sweat shirt, with her back against the head of the bed. "Come and sit by me, Daiki."

"Please forgive me, Debra.," he blurted out.

"Daiki, there is no need to forgive. We both need to find our peace in whatever relationship we hope to have. I wouldn't have you any other way than the way you are, honest about your fears and limits. But I want so much to try. I've missed you since that last time we were together."

They held hands while they began discussing their future. They would give themselves all the time they needed to know each other well, before making any commitments. Daiki wanted to be sure Debra could enjoy Japanese life and his family in particular. His family didn't have any extra space in the house, but they would find room and, at least, his parents wouldn't worry that they were alone there, when they shouldn't be. They'd never be alone in his household of fourteen people in five rooms.

Debra wanted to be sure that she would be strong, would not find a need for drugs again. Since she would be living in a new land, she couldn't foresee what circumstances might frighten or weaken her.

She had planned to live in Japan for awhile, so his home would be the best place for them to start out. She thought that the tight living space in his home would be a good experience for her. Anyway, she wasn't used to living in luxury. His parents could introduce her to the Buddhist temple and the family traditions. Daiki would work in Japan as he had planned. Since he had somewhat acculturated to America, they could move there for a job or a life-change if that ever became necessary.

If Barry agreed, he could go on to Kobe as planned. That would give Daiki and Debra a week or so to be alone with Daiki's family. Debra and Daiki would meet him at the Kobe port. They could see a little of Kobe with him while all three decided on Barry's future. Would he come with them to Yokohama, stay and work in Kobe or return to the United States and back to his job there.

Though they had said they weren't ready to talk about marriage yet, it wasn't long before they couldn't avoid what was already in their hearts. They would be married in a full Buddhist ceremony. As Daiki described the ceremony, Debra was enthralled.

First the monks, who stayed up the entire night before the wedding to pray, would chant, then receive an offering. The bride and groom would sit on the floor with hands folded in lotus position, while each received a crown of flowers on their head. Their crowns would be tied together with string. Then rings would be exchanged and their hands washed by pouring water over their hands into a bowl of flowers, the sign of the beauty, purity and enlightenment they would be bringing to one another's lives, to their marriage, their children and their community.

They talked long into the night, interrupted occasionally by affectionate hugs and kisses. Barry eventually turned in on Don's extra bed.

The next day, the short wave radio that Barry brought finally kicked in its first message. The eleven travelers in the lounge hollered hoopla over their first communication with land: first they heard a broadcast from Russia playing American rock and roll, then the prices of vegetables in Japan, as translated for them by Daiki while Debra struggled to learn the words in, what she was thinking of as, her new language. Radio reception meant they were near the first port where they could disembark while the freight was unloaded.

Yokohama was now only two days off. Debra and Daiki were energized, their time completely occupied with packing, planning and language lessons. Debra wanted to be able to greet Daiki's parents in perfect Japanese when she met them. Barry was in total agreement with their plan.

The night before docking they all stayed up until 11o'clock hoping to see land but there was too much fog. At 4:30 in the morning they were startled awake by a jarring of the ship. They had reached port. They looked out of their portholes to see that they had bumped into a huge army vessel that was anchored next to them. Land at last!

Debra and Daiki joined the others for breakfast as the ship was not yet anchored at the dock for them to alight. Their suitcases were waiting at the top of the ramp. As soon as it was extended they hugged everyone aboard. "We'll see you next week at the Kobe dock," they said excitedly as down the ramp they hurried.

The other passengers watched Debra and Daiki reach the bottom of the ramp. They were met by Daiki's parents and all five of his siblings. The younger ones were jumping up and down, totally ignoring Debra, they were so excited to see him.

Daiki, put his arm around Debra and proudly introduced her, first to his parents, then the others. Each person in turn beginning with Dad, folded their own hands in lotus position and gave a slight bow and smile.

"Oh how I wish I could hear what Daiki is saying to them," Lillian said excitedly.

"I don't think they need his words," Goose said. "He looks so proud of her."

It's going to be okay, it seemed to all their shipmates, Debra and Daiki's ship family. They were all feeling torn though, relieved, utterly happy for the pair, but experiencing the first loss of part of their family. Liesl and Don quietly took each others hands as they watched the scene below. Goose noticed and walked over to Allie and Priscilla, pried himself between them and took each by the hand. Lillian clapped heartily. Beverly, Barry and Ethel stood together, big grins on their faces. Then, seeming to need time alone to deal with all the emotions of that moment in their own way, they began to disperse.

Eventually they showed up again, one by one, on the port side of the ship to watch it unload. They watched the huge cranes from their ship drop crates into small wooden Japanese vessels. After about two hours and the thrilling expectation of seeing Japan, they couldn't wait to get on land. Most planned to tour the port city, their first experience of Asia, together, and return to the ship for dinner. Lillian passed on this excursion in favor of painting the scene of port life and portraits of some of the characters there. She was already busy with her sketch pad and had an easel and paints set up on the deck when they disembarked.

During their days anchored at the Yokohama port they toured its city and countryside. They ate squid and seaweed, they attended a Japanese tea party, where Liesl said, her face muscles hurt from so much smiling and so many "arigatos". They rode the world's fastest train through rice fields, sweet potato and onion fields and saw rows and rows of bamboo clothes lines where the hand washed clothes were hung. In the distance, they could see an ancient castle on a green hill that was flanked by a black mountain range. On this train adventure they found that this was a mysterious, varied and exciting land.

On the way back to the ship on the last day they almost missed departure time. They were stopped by student demonstrations against the presence of American aggression. The demonstrators wanted American "security forces," out of Japan. Thousands of well organized demonstrators had met near their dock where the California Bear was anchored. They waved placards: "Stop the killing" or "Americans go home". They were chanting in Japanese rhythm and melody, words that the passengers didn't understand but the message was clear. The travelers were afraid of pushing their American faces through this crowd. Goose took over.

"Everybody hold hands. I'll go first and pull you through. Don, you take the middle, hold onto Priscilla and Liesl and Barry you hang on at the rear. Let's go!"

All of the jostling was frightening but they arrived on board safely, to find their lounge turned into an art gallery. Lillian had even painted a scene of the demonstrators near the ship ramp. She was full of stories and couldn't wait until she would disembark at the next port, Kobe. It then would be a week since they had said adieu to Debra and Daiki.

* * *

When the ship did dock at Kobe, Debra and Daiki were waiting there for Barry. The other passengers alighted with him to give their hugs to Debra and Daiki.

Debra handed a brown paper package, tied with string, to Liesl and said, "Open this when no one else is around."

Goose pulled Daiki aside. "Tell me the truth Kid. Is it all right with your family?"

Daiki was elated. "Goose, my brothers and sisters love Debra. Soon my parents will too. I can feel it. My mom gives her language lessons every day and claps every time Debra says something correctly. My dad proudly introduces her to everyone as "our friend".

"We haven't talked with them about marriage yet, of course, but we will when the time is right. I know now that it will never matter that our eyes and skin are different or that her hair is sandy and mine is black or that we've come to this day by different routes."

"But what about all those things you were so worried about?" Goose asked. "Does it seem that they will upset your father?"

"Her past will never interfere with our love or our admiration for each other," Daiki said. "Debra did the right thing by telling me about her son right in the beginning. It took courage for her. I'm the one who was the weakling, but that is behind us now. What Debra and I have together is openness and calmness, it is life. It is our whole being. We know each other's soul, we find our peace at the same source. We can come back to that source in any struggle." He took Goose's hand, not knowing how to express himself strongly enough. "Goose, thank you. If it wasn't for you..."

"Heck, I knew you had it in you Kid," Goose said. Then he added, "This is the first time I ever hugged a man so hard." Goose quickly turned to climb the ramp before his happy tears could overcome him, ruin his image. Young love is strong and wonderful, Goose was thinking. Fact, een when it's not so young, it can overcome anything that wants to get in its way. May it last forever, theirs and ours.

Liesl couldn't wait to see what was in the package that Debra had given her, so, at her first chance she climbed the ramp and went into Debra and Barry's empty room and shut the door. Inside the package was a note, "Have a happy life, Liesl. You might need these." The package contained a few of Debra's clothes: tennis shoes and sandals, an Irish wool sweater, a pair of jeans, a pair of shorts and several blouses. Liesl repackaged it and hid it in the closet formerly belonging to Debra. Yes, she would be needing these things. Debra knew.

Hoping her absence hadn't been noticed, Liesl went back on land to join Lillian, Don, Priscilla and Allie, who would be seeing more of Japan together. Soon Goose returned too, face wiped dry and ready for adventure. "Let's take a taxi ride," Liesl pleaded.

Goose, who was experienced with Asian cities, laughed. "Sure Liesl. You'll love the experience."

They all five piled into the first taxi that stopped for them. The road was filled with autos, bicycles, motorcycles, pedestrians. At intersections, no lights were obeyed, everyone in any vehicle or no vehicle just kept moving in at least six directions, sometimes perpendicular to the traffic lane. They finally arrived at a more rural area where surely the drive would be safer.

Here the street was one lane wide but used for two-way traffic. If a vehicle from the other direction got in the way, the taxi driver honked forcefully, made a forty-five degree turn around the approaching one and kept going. There were lots of honks and swerves.

"I'm just going to close my eyes, hold my breath and feel the wind as we zoom," cried Lillian.

"Let's go back to town and see a department store," suggested Liesl. When they arrived at the department store in town it was almost closing time. All the merchants had begun to holler or bellow in an attempt to sell their wares before the store closed. The racket continued until the store's doors were locked.

"Tomorrow I want to ride a train again," Don said. "I loved being among the mobs of Japanese people, a great place to observe their culture."

"I have a surprise for you tomorrow," Goose said. "We must be at my friend's house, right near the dock, by five o'clock."

The next day they boarded the train early. As before, they watched fascinated, as men and women boarded, found a seat, took off their shoes and squatted on the seats. Some changed their clothes on the train to put on something lighter because the train was hot. One mother told her little boy to bow to the foreigners. The child knew how to bow, but did so in the wrong direction so that all they saw was his little rear end.

Then Lillian's favorite, whom she talked about and laughed about for days. "This very sophisticated looking Japanese gentleman boarded the train, probably going to work. He was dressed in a full tailored navy blue suit, white shirt, tie, leather shoes and carried a brief case. He came to his seat, put down the brief case, took off his leather shoes, unbuckled his belt, unzipped and removed his trousers, folded them neatly and hung them over the seat back. Then, wearing only his shorts, he jumped up on the seat, squatted and took out his economic journal to study on his way to work. The funniest part was that no one noticed him doing all that. I wonder what Debra will say when Daiki tries it," she laughed.

"What a great blend of East and West in one man," Allie said.

After unsuccessfully begging Goose to give them hints of the surprise he had waiting for them, they finally arrived by taxi at the port side before five o'clock.

Goose was howling. "If I told you what we are going to do now you might not have come, but here you are. Just follow me. You'll see why I liked having a girl in every port."

They weaved their way through local people, men holding hands, nude babies, women in kimonos, squatting children playing with stones for marbles. They soon arrived at a row of attached townhouses lining both sides of a narrow street. Goose's friend was waiting outside her open door.

"This is my friend Akiko," Goose began, and to Akiko, "These are my friends from the ship, Lillian, Don, Liesl, Allie and Priscilla." Akiko was dressed in a pink and lavender kimono and had her black hair tied up with small bamboo sticks. She wore open sandals which she slipped off as she entered her doorway. Each American clumsily took off their shoes as they entered her house. Akiko bowed at each in turn and they attempted to copy her.

"Akiko will give you the experience of a Japanese bath. She has warmed the water for you in advance. That takes her several hours because she draws the water and places one bucket at a time on her stove to heat it. Akiko, show our friends where you heat your water."

Akiko took them into her kitchen. She had a small gas stove with an iron burner and also a small open pit fireplace. She pointed to the open pit. "She can heat more water here so it doesn't take as long." Goose helped.

She then took them to the bathing room. It was about six feet by six feet with cement floor. One corner was built up about three feet and was three by three feet square, the "tub" which Akiko had filled with heated water. Goose gave directions in English while Akiko demonstrated.

"You go into the bathing room, remove your clothes and use the soap or one of those stones and this bowl for water to scrub your body. She showed them a metal bowl the size of a dog bowl. When you have finished you get into the tub to rinse off and soak. Be sure you don't pull the plug out when you are finished soaking because everyone has to use the same water to rinse in.

"Who wants to go first?"

Allie grabbed at the chance. She'd be the first to soak in that tub. Priscilla refused to join her. She wanted the same experience as the others, alone in the bathing room. All would have to use the same water. She was followed by Priscilla, Lillian, then Liesl, then Don.

"Goose, your turn," Don called when he was finished.

"Aw, heck, I've done it a hundred times," Goose said, and he sat back down with his cup of tea, looked at his watch and reminded, "We better get back to the ship now. They might want to pull out tonight."

Laughing, hooting, giggling and clean, the five travelers bowed to Akiko, said their best "arigato" and followed Goose to the ship, Don and Liesl holding hands, Allie hitting Goose on the shoulder good naturedly.

"Goose, I can't believe you did that to us," Allie said, teasingly.

"First time I took a bath in four other people's water, Don added.

"It won't be the last if you intend to bathe while you're in Asia. And now, if the weather stays warm enough to keep the water warm, Akiko, and maybe some of her friends, will use your water for at least another week," Goose said.

Chapter 19

ARRIVAL IN PUSAN

It took only one day to reach the port of Pusan, Korea and what an important day that was.

"Don," Liesl looked around the lounge, no privacy could be counted on here. "Can we go someplace?" He took her hand and pulled her toward his room. "No not there." Liesl was afraid. She wouldn't be able to hold back, to have a proper conversation in that much privacy. He then pulled her toward the two chairs on the aft of the fourth deck.

"Don, tell me how you feel about me and if you think we could have a future together. We have had so little time together, without nine other people looking over our shoulders. Yet, I'm about to make the most important decision of my life. Romance is all so new to me. I have to know more clearly if I'm experiencing love or infatuation. I have to know about you too, what are your intentions? You've been urging me to be with you more, but is it just a ship romance you want?"

"Liesl, love is always complex and simple. It's hard for me to explain but not hard for me to know. When I first watched you in the sunset under the Golden Gate Bridge, I knew it would be love. I have lusted after other women in my thirty years, but you are different.

"I know your purpose. You are traveling to a strange people and country to help those whom no one else is helping. You are bringing them, not only care but the knowledge of how to treat their illness so that one day it will be cured. You're excited about learning from them too. You've been studying their language. You understand that more primitive people have so much to teach us.

"You aren't trying to entice anyone. You just welcome everyone. You don't flirt with your eyes; you express the warmth that anyone could snuggle in. And since I first saw you, I have seen you open up to the gifts of others. Even the sea. You love the sea, its brightness and its storminess equally. You watch the sea without fear. Except, of course, you often avoid watching it with me. You avoid doing much of anything too close to me. I seem to frighten you. I seem to be the only one that makes you flinch, run away.

"Liesl, I think you run from me whenever we get too close. I think you love me and are afraid of love. Most of all, I know that I love you. I love you enough that if you choose to follow your original plan I will be sad but I will turn and walk away from you to free you.

"Liesl, you and I can get off this ship together in Vietnam. We can work together for the street kids, give them the mother love and father help that I could never give them alone. Wouldn't that fulfill your purpose?"

Liesl nodded. She knew it made sense but it was so much to process.

Don continued. "I can't promise that you'll never be lonely and you may be poor. But, Liesl, I can promise I'll love you always. I have an intense desire for you, your body as well as your soul. I can't live near you as if you are a nun. If you come with me, we will be intimate with each other and if you will have me, we will be husband and wife."

They were both fully aroused, their longing intense. It was all so new for Liesl. She had always squelched such feelings. Now she was giving them full rein. Don grabbed Liesl and kissed her passionately. She fell into his arms, weak kneed, pulled off her veil, returned his kiss with open eyes and longing. Finally, it was Liesl who pulled away and sat down.

"Yes, Don, I want you with all my heart. I feel sure of that now, but..."

"Liesl, if you don't want for us to be completely immersed in one another, I'll need to stay away from you for the rest of this trip, because my whole body fills with an electric charge when I'm with you. I will respect you always, but I know myself. It has to be all or none."

Liesl pondered her future. The whole of it seemed to pass before her in a moment: *The Vietnamese children would fulfill my purpose beautifully. I love Don so much, I'm ecstatic about being with him. I will be blessed to have him to teach me and be at my side in this exciting unexpected detour of my life's journey. This will be my new mission, the new place and people with whom I'll find the same God I've always sought.*

"I'll come to Vietnam with you and love you with my whole body and soul," she said almost shyly. After a moment she added, "But Don, we have another week on this ship. I need to figure out my transition. I need to think and pray about it. Please be patient with me this next week."

Don stood again, took her in his arms, held her tightly. He was as dazed as she was, with the awareness of what had just happened to their lives. Again, Liesl was the one who had to pull away from their embrace. If she stayed any longer they would end up in his room together and she wasn't ready for that.

Later that beautiful evening she leaned on the ship rail and meditated on her life's path. She had always loved time to be alone, time for her mind to be blank, when even reflecting would interfere with her mood. But now when she was alone it was different. Now she had experienced the exhilaration of hearty laughter and good friends. Now she knew what she had been missing for the thirteen years of her adulthood. Now her aloneness was interrupted, not by the urge to get her work done as before, not by the demands of people in need or the call of her prayer schedule. This was different. It was the call to give time to laughter, love, cheer, beauty. And the hard part, the need for time to make difficult decisions and choices. Never again would anyone else be making those choices for her.

Now aloneness compelled her to something more pressing. It meant days, hours, minutes before she could express her love. Watching the beautiful sunset over the waters, she suddenly realized how disconnected she was feeling from all the people in her life who mattered so much to her, the people she had shoved away in order to protect her vocation, her family and now Don. Only crossing the water as swiftly as that sun was setting would relieve the urgency, the ardor in her heart.

She still had to deal with the practical things. The fear of losing everything that she had committed her life to so long ago was still pervading her feelings. The timing. When would she make the final change, on the ship or later? Could she leave Ethel to work in Thailand alone? Who did she have to inform of her decision, and when? Did she really want to be a wife, a mother, to belong, in a sense, to someone else?

In the morning Liesl awoke from a dream which was so real that she had to sit up and review it for awhile to be sure she wouldn't forget it. In her dream she was in her mother's kitchen sitting on one of the bright red naugahyde chairs with chrome legs. Her mom was cooking, as always, turning between the gas burners and chrome and white formica table. Her mom said something to her that seemed very important, then she looked up and blew, and the roof flew off the house. Suddenly, Liesl's chair started to float upwards but she realized when she was quite high over the house, that she couldn't go any further because her chair was tied to her mother's apron strings. Her mother called 'go with my blessing' and Liesl wanted to fly far but she couldn't go any further because of those apron strings.

The message of her dream seemed so clear to Liesl. It was time to cut the strings that kept her from full flight. The values she had received from her mother included freedom from her childhood ideals, or rather, her mother seemed to want her to live her ideals to their fullest. Liesl got up and out of bed. Ethel was already out of the room. She looked out of the porthole. They were in Pusan, Korea.

Chapter 20

LILLIAN IN PUSAN

Pusan, Korea. Lillian would finally get off this ship and work with the poor port-side children. Even Japan didn't compare to Pusan. Loud, busy, using the most primitive equipment to unload the ship. The dinghies in the harbor looked like one would picture Noah's Arc with every kind of critter aboard. A bulk bag of one hundred pounds of sugar broke as it was being unloaded. It poured down over the sweaty men in the dinghy sticking to everyone and everything. In America we would have said, "What a mess!" and quickly washed off the stickiness. But not in Pusan. The men started licking off all they could of the sugar. They stuffed it in their pockets. Kids jumped on board the dinghies. They ripped off their tee shirts and turned them into sacks.

Little girls carrying water home dumped the water and filled their containers with sugar. Within minutes all of the sugar was gone.

The passengers were so fascinated with the scene that they hesitated to leave the ship and go to town. They had been informed that the ship was scheduled to be in this port for five days so they would have many opportunities to tour Korea. Lillian, waiting to alight, had all the musical instruments she could manage in two big plastic garbage bags, kazoos, harmonicas, a few small drum sets and horns, but she was laughing so hard at the sugar escapades that she couldn't start walking. Don was ready with his camera and kept shooting.

"Wouldn't that have been a wonderful scene for Daiki to write about," he said. "I'll do the best I can with my camera and send it to him."

"Well here I go," said Lillian, lugging her bags.

"Lillian, you can't just get off a ship in Pusan, Korea where you don't know the language and create a band with those begging children," Beverly chided.

"If you want something enough, kindness and joy will be all the language you need," Lillian said as she started down the gang plank with abandon.

Don grabbed Liesl by the hand and pulled her behind him to follow Lillian. "I know she wants to go alone but let's follow her a little way to see how she's doing and be sure she's safe."

Lillian turned and saw them. "Now don't you worry about me. I've been wanting to do this all my life. It doesn't matter if it's Pusan, Korea or Concord, California. You'll see." When she reached the bottom of the gang plank, three eight-year-olds who clearly didn't speak English ran up to her and held out their hands.

"Soap please, soap please." Miraculously, Lillian produced several bars of soap. "Cigarette please, thank you," one said.

Lillian put her arm around the shoulder of that boy and said excitedly, "Look what I have for you." She dug into her bag and pulled out a drum and drumsticks. "Please help me find some more boys." She held open her plastic bag so they could look inside. They all oohed and aahed.

She looked like the Pied Piper, twenty kids following her. The last Don and Liesl saw of her, she was walking in the fish market between aisles. By that time three of the boys were blowing horns and more were gathering. She was talking up a storm and they, who knew no English, understood her perfectly.

By the time the travelers reached Pusan, they had become courageous enough to head out into the town in smaller numbers. Don and Liesl started walking up the crowded street away from the port. "Let's hail a cab," Don suggested. "Maybe the driver will know where to take us."

"Will it be anything like the Japanese taxi?" Liesl giggled.

They had studied important words in their translation dictionaries, especially the words for money and bargaining. Don knew from experience that one is expected to bargain for everything in Asia. The requested price is never what the entrepreneur really expects one to pay. This was their first challenge in Korea. Since they didn't know how to tell their driver where they wanted to go, they decided not to try to bargain for the price but to just pay what was asked.

They hailed a cab and pointed up the hill. It was raining lightly. The little cab, a real automobile, started up the steep hill, began to sputter, then smoke, then it stopped. Shopkeepers, children without shoes, a pregnant woman, other women with babies on their backs, Fu Manchu beards poured out of the shops to offer advice and help. The taxi driver went into a shop and returned with a bucket of water, lifted the hood of the car and dumped the water over the engine. Now a boy appeared, who had one leg and was using a small tree limb for a crutch. He knew a few words of English and finally understood. The Americans want to go to town where there are restaurants, church, market, stores.

The taxi still would not start. The water hadn't helped. "We will walk," Liesl told them as she started to get out of the taxi. A long conversation between the taxi driver and the translator ensued. "No, the Americans must ride," the translator said and all the people were in agreement. Eventually the whole town helped push the taxi up the steep hill about four blocks with Don and Liesl riding ashamedly.

Pusan, Korea looked very poor. The streets were muddy and narrow, the buses were very old, the taxi's were struggling to run, shops were tiny. In a hardware shop, bicycles were soldered. In the basket store, jute was braided. in the clothing store threads were woven. Don and Liesl ate noodles in a shop where the rice was crushed and formed into noodles. Babies were carried on backs and young children were sometimes nude. School children were in uniform. They visited a Church where Liesl determined she would bring Ethel the next day along with anyone else who wanted to come. Then before dinner they returned to the ship. No taxi this time, walking back downhill would be a preferable.

Back on ship, dinner conversation was full of the day's adventure. Goose had gone off with Allie and Priscilla, Ethel and Beverly had gone together, Lillian though alone, had returned safely and excited about the next day. They agreed that it would be a good idea for them to return to the ship for dinner each day to ensure that they all were safe.

The next morning at five o'clock, Ethel, Liesl and Beverly started their walk up hill to the church for Mass. The church was directly across from a hospital. The three women crossed the street after the service to view the hospital. It had been established by French Sisters and so looked very much like a European or American Hospital of an earlier time. With twenty-patient wards, there was one bathroom per floor from which water was carried as needed. But unlike western hospitals, it had squat toilets built into the floor. A Korean administrator who spoke some English toured the women through the hospital. Then they returned to the ship.

On board they tuned in the short-wave radio that Barry had left for them as a gift. They received a broadcast from Radio Peking titled, "Down with Imperialist America." The beautiful musical compositions each carried similar titles: "Long Live Chinese Revolutionaries" and "Overcome the Evils of Imperialism." Beverly was frightened but Liesl and Ethel felt certain that their American crewmen would not put them into danger.

The third day Lillian announced that she would not be returning to the ship that night and the others were not to worry about her. She had an appointment with the American consulate and they would put her up in a nearby hotel. The others could not pry the story from her. How did Lillian arrange this?

"You will see when we're ready to leave Korea," was all she would say.

"We have to trust her," Goose said. "She's already done the impossible with those children."

"Maybe they're going to buy her art work," Liesl suggested.

"Or hire her band," Beverly cackled.

The next day it was pouring rain making it necessary for the ship hold to remain closed and delaying their schedule. The fourth day it poured again, adding another day to their stay in Korea, which would now be a whole week long. Lillian left the ship despite the rain.

She was met at the bottom of the ramp by an American jeep. Something was up with her.

On the sixth evening in Korea, Lillian arrived back at the ship with the announcement: "I am going to have a child."

Goose hee hawed. "Lillian! we know you'd have no trouble seducing a man, but at age seventy..."

Lillian's words tumbled one over the other. "I can't wait to tell you all so you just be quiet and listen to me. The first day we were in Pusan, the children took me to see this little girl and her mom who was very sick. Hana, the little girl, her name means flower, is eight years old. Her father was American and was stationed in Korea as security officer after the end of the war. He died before Hana was born. Her mother is Korean and has terminal cancer. They have no other relatives here.

"When her mom first realized that she would die, she applied for a Passport for Hana. She said she had always hoped that Hana could go to America someday but the father's family didn't want her, so Mom didn't know how it could happen. Hana already speaks a little English because her mom has been preparing her for this. So, with Hana translating, her mom asked me to take the child.

"Well I have all my paperwork with me, of course, you know, passport and all, so the people at the outreach consulate were able to establish whatever they need to about me. So I said, 'yes, I'd love to have Hana.' Even though I'm old, I'll be like her grandma, I have all those grandchildren and we can make a very happy home for Hana.

"I haven't told Jerry yet, of course. I can't wait to tell him he's going to be a father. He can start studying the Korean language right now. He'll be getting two of us for the price of one. He'll be so excited."

"It will be very hard for Hana to lose her mom of course, but she's known for a long time that America is what her mom wants for her, and it might be a little easier because she already loves me."

Allie asked, "Lillian, will you stay in Korea or fly back with Hana or bring her on the ship?"

"Well of course, that is the hard part for me. I will miss you all so much, but Hana needs me. The doctors say it should only be a month or so until her mom dies. I must stay here for her, and we can work on the formal adoption papers during that month. The councilor from the Embassy outreach program in Pusan has already signed a good faith statement assigning Hana to me. We'll probably fly home to San Francisco after her mom's death."

Beverly chided, "Of all people on this ship that I thought would have a little sense! What has happened to you? All of you mature people have been transformed on this ship. It's like your lives were at sea and now you've all gone crazy finding new beginnings."

Lillian motioned Beverly over to her. "Which reminds me Bev, I promised to help you think about a new project for yourself. I have a wonderful idea that we need to talk about in private."

Beverly was doubtful. "Just don't come up with any hare-brained ideas like me having another child."

From here on, the lounge was abuzz with everyone talking at the same time. Lillian pulled Beverly aside for a protracted conversation which the others noted, was punctuated by many exclamations.

The next morning at dawn, the jeep was back, waiting by the gangplank for Lillian. Beverly, Ethel, Liesl, Don, Goose, Allie and Priscilla walked down the gangplank ahead of her each carrying a sack of toys, soap, musical instruments and Lillian's own suitcase. After loading the bags in the jeep, there were many hugs and tears before she jumped into the front passenger side. They were waving long after the jeep was out of sight, then, each absorbed in thought, climbed back up the ramp as the ship was tooting farewell to Korea.

Chapter 21

THE MOON

It was July sixteenth on the Asian Pacific blue, July fifteenth in America. This was an important day, not just for America, but for the entire world, even out in the ocean off the coast of Vietnam. Before the end of the day, at 2130 Asian time, the Apollo eleven mission would launch, headed for the moon carrying three American astronauts. There was an added excitement on this ship for one of its passengers, Alexis Clause, had been instrumental in creating the flag which would be placed on the moon by Neil Armstrong.

As evening approached a storm was blowing up. By 2100 it was whipping the California Bear. The ship swayed, rocked, jerked, sometimes crashed from side to side, wave to wave. The passengers, now only seven of them were dizzy, some of them sick, their stomachs heaving along with the ship. As the storm unbalanced the freighter, they held on to the nailed-down table in the passenger lounge.

Don was manning their short wave radio, intent on hearing the launch of Apollo. He tuned with increasingly clumsy hands hearing only static. It was only ten minutes to launch time now. It was dark and raining. The iron steps that spiraled the mast were slippery. "I'm going up the steps to a higher spot," Don announced. "I will see if I can get better reception up there.

"I'm going with you," Liesl insisted. I want so badly to hear the launching.

"I'm dying to hear it," Allie said, "but I don't dare leave my mom after what happened last time I left her."

"You should go if you want to Allie. I'll keep my arm around Priscilla while you're gone and she'll be just fine." Goose felt like, as the strong one here, he should be accompanying Don, but Allie was the most important person on this occasion, so his place was with Priscilla.

Don, Allie and Liesl put on their windbreakers, stepped out into the rain and started up the wet iron steps. Don held onto the rail with one hand and the radio with the other. The ladies held the rail with both hands, walking ahead of Don. Stepping cautiously, their feet could not keep up with their excitement, their eyes stretched upward as if looking for the spaceship which was still on the ground across the sea in America. Out there, across the black ocean, the men inside Columbia were waiting for the same count down that Liesl, Don and Allie awaited. As they reached the top of the steps, the drenching rain and driving wind was of little importance compared to the voice that came along with the static from the shortwave radio, "10...9...8...7..." When the announcer shouted "one" it felt to them as if their bodies blasted them into the air along with Apollo eleven.

The exhilaration of the moment lasted for many moments, then they turned to descend the iron steps. Don, Liesl and Allie still tightly holding the rail had forgotten their fear of losing hold of being washed into the waves. When they returned to the lounge the other passengers cheered their arrival as if they had just come back from the moon itself.

As the thrill of that historical moment subsided the passengers one-by-one turned in to their rooms leaving only Don and Liesl in the lounge. The rain had stopped, leaving bluish rays coming in to the windows. Liesl looked at Don, then grabbed his hand and said,

"Come on, it must be moon rays. Let's go see them."

They climbed the iron steps again, this time holding only each other. The dark clouds had dissipated enough for them to see the full moon. It was just hanging there awaiting the space ship Columbia's visit. This was the first time since they met that they had been truly alone with no fear of an intrusion.

Don looked out at the sea. The clouds had dissipated and all of the stars of the milky way were shining. Don pulled Liesl tighter. He was about to say "Liesl, I love you" to her, but when he saw the longing in her eyes, he couldn't speak. He pulled her downward on the steps toward their fourth deck. It was a moment Liesl could not have planned, but when the time came for him to lead her away she didn't resist.

She couldn't feel her feet beneath her. She floated, almost bounced along, like a dry leaf on a rushing river. Nothing entered her mind except the unity with Don that she longed for. It felt to her like an invisible line pulled her along to wherever he was going. She felt nothing more until her feet touched the floor of his cabin, and she heard his door close behind her. As Don quickly and gently pulled one piece of her clothing off after another, she felt the coolness of the air on her body that longed for the heat of his.

As Don undressed, Liesl experienced that terrible eternal second of ambivalence when she wanted to look at his naked body forever, but could not wait to make it one with her own. It was like there was no way to be close enough to him unless she could climb inside of him, or him in her.

After a first total possession, Don ripped the bed linens off of both beds onto the floor so that they could lie on the cushioned floor and move without spacial or time limit. After a long time, she didn't know how long, Liesl fell briefly asleep but the movement of his body, again awakened and aroused them both. Falling asleep a second time, she turned away from him, then awoke to feel him searching again until, his arms wrapped around her waist, he took her to paradise once more. They wanted the fireworks and the serenity of that night to last forever.

In the morning, Don, at Liesl's request, retrieved the package from Debra's room. Also as Liesl asked him to, he knocked on Ethel's door. "I have something I must tell you," he said to her. "I have a message from Liesl." He then told her that Liesl felt it would be disingenuous of her to continue walking around wearing a nun's habit. Not to shock Ethel, Liesl wanted her to know in advance that this morning she would be wearing jeans when she came to breakfast. Then he returned to his cabin and to Liesl.

As he watched Liesl dress, Don was excited by her every move. He realized that he had never seen her wearing pink. Pretty, how it illuminated her pink cheeks. And how her dark brown hair accented the color of her eyes. When they could tear themselves apart long enough, they came to breakfast together, Liesl wearing her new jeans, a pink blouse, Irish sweater and sandals. Her dark hair was bobbed.

Allie, Goose and Priscilla greeted Don and Liesl with hugs.

"I love you both," Priscilla said.

"I'm so happy for you," Allie said.

"And will you, Liesl, be getting off in Vietnam?" Goose asked.

Liesl grabbed Priscilla and hugged her, then turned to all the others. "Yes, Don and I will be getting off together in Haiphong, Vietnam. Each of you has contributed more than you will ever know to my decision, and to the happiness that Don and I share, now. We do not know how long we'll be here. It depends a lot on how long the war lasts and on our ability to help Harlan, Don's friend here, provide for the Vietnamese children. We pray that some day we will be blessed with our own children as well."

Don looked wordlessly at his ship family, looked at Liesl and pulled her close. As they stood there together, Don, who found it hard to speak to any group, couldn't let his feelings for them all go unspoken. "How could I ask for more? I am overwhelmed by your love, by the gift of Liesl and by the work before us. Thank you all for your part in our lives."

Ethel managed to say nothing.

Beverly chimed in, "Lillian suggested I might be able to help Ethel in Thailand. You, Liesl, leaving this ship with Don instead of with Ethel, makes everything perfect, because if you're not going with Ethel to Thailand she'll really need me. She already said I can come with her. Wait til Alma and Albert hear what I'm going to do."

"And you thought everyone except yourself was at sea," Goose said to Beverly. "Now who is it that's gone crazy?"

And so breakfast ended on an upbeat, lighthearted note despite Ethel's discomfort with the whole scenario.

Captain Mack joined them at breakfast. For the third time, he had had to arrange for different departure sites for passengers, than had been reserved. First Debra getting off in Yokohama instead of Kobe, then Lillian, a total surprise, disembarking in Pusan, and now Liesl in Haiphong.

When he arrived in the dining room he took one look at Liesl, then looked up and down her, smiling broadly. "Well," he said and winked at her. Then he addressed the group. "For such a small group I can make my announcement right here. We will be docking in Haiphong, South Vietnam at about 1000 hours today. As you know, due to the war, we will not be able to allow passengers to alight here, with the exception of Mr. Renick and Ms. Victorine who will be remaining here in Vietnam. We will not extend the gang plank, as a helicopter, which will bring several new passengers to the ship and take Mr. Renick and Ms. Victorine to land, will be landing on our stern. We will be in this port only the few hours needed to remove supplies needed by our men stationed here."

Beverly spoke up, "Captain Mack, I have something I have to say to you. I will be getting off the ship in Bangkok, not in The Netherlands as planned. How will I arrange for that?"

Captain Mack sat down, rested his elbow on the table and put his hand to his forehead and shook his head. "I guess I shouldn't be surprised, should I? Beverly, come and see me after we leave Vietnam.

"This has been the most ungodly fickle group I've ever traveled with."

Goose offered, "Captain Mack, don't worry about our numbers because I'm not getting off in Manila as planned. I'm going to Rotterdam, The Netherlands with Allie and Priscilla. So Beverly and I can kinda change places."

"Good," Captain Mack answered. "Instead of buying tickets for specific ports, why didn't you all just play scramble or fifty-two pickup at the beginning of this voyage. Without making reservations, you would have all landed in the right places. Goose, you come and see me too, but please don't come with Beverly. You'll confuse me too much."

"Captain Mack, may Liesl and I leave this meeting now?" Don asked. "We're kind of in a hurry."

Don and Liesl had little time to pack their things after breakfast.. Liesl was leaving her nun's uniform with Ethel and managed to get her few other things into Don's small bags. Don and Liesl said 'goodbye' to their fellow passengers with many hugs and good wishes but no address exchanges. No one knew where they would be living next. When all was said and done they hurried back through the wind to stand on the stern of the ship where the helicopter was going to land, hoping that Harlan would be waiting on shore. They all stood back and held on to each other as the landing helicopter-produced wind unsteadied them.

When the copter had landed, Don grabbed Liesl by the hand and pulled her to the port side of the ship. He wanted to survey the shore before alighting, and there he saw Harlan, standing watching the ship and copter. He had three little boys by the hands. Harlan was waving. The boys were jumping up and down with excitement, just as Lillian's grandchildren were when they boarded the ship in America, a small world and a whole lifetime ago. What a journey this had been for Don and Liesl, and it was only beginning. Harlan of course, was expecting only Don, but Don was certain that he would find room for Liesl in his quarters, wherever they were.

"Don't be concerned about that" Liesl smiled, "We can always find room on the floor."

As they boarded the helicopter they turned to wave their farewell to the shrinking ship family but Goose and Allie and Priscilla and Ethel and Beverly were all engrossed in greeting the new passengers that had just boarded. A new journey was beginning for all of them.

EPILOGUE

Binh took his place on one of the forty leather seats that were attached around the periphery of the shuttle. He had plenty of time yet before he would be required to buckle up the harness that held shoulders, forehead, even feet in place during lift-off. Only ones arms were left free, to keep you from feeling claustrophobic or restrained. He had promised himself after that first outer-space flight that he would make a trip every few years either to a space station or to the moon. There was no thrill that could match this one and it was so easily available now.

Binh watched the other passengers climb aboard and receive directions from the host stationed at the open hatch. He started imagining their stories as he watched them enter. That must be a golden anniversary couple. I wonder if its their daughter and son-in-law or son and daughter-in-law with them. Its gotta be their son; he looks just like his dad. Oh, look at that baby, only about ten years old. I wonder if he is flying alone. Presently a thirty-year-old-ish attractive bright-eyed woman with a bonnet of black curls boarded. As he watched the host give her directions he noticed that she was being directed to the seat beside him. Oh, this is my lucky day, he thought.

She walked over to the empty place next to him, took her seat, looked around the craft, then looked at Binh with big blue excited eyes. "This is my first flight," she said. "I'm so thrilled to be going, but I'm scared too."

"Will it help if I describe to you what it will be like? Or will that make it worse?" he asked.

"Oh, please do," she responded quickly.

"Well, first they will have us buckle-up. These harnesses keep you in your seat during lift-off. They go around your ankles, waist, shoulders and forehead. I'll show you when the time comes. You'll be able to see everything from your seat. Just watch the windows across from us. See those ceiling mirrors? They will reflect everything that you can't see directly. They will reflect the earth as we take off so that you can see its shape as we lift higher and higher. That is the most amazing part of this whole trip. To think that you can see your earth, even the shape of our continent and then the whole world!

"When you're back home after having been on the moon, you'll think you've been having visions; you'll think it was your imagination. Who wouldn't have visions? You will have seen the earth looking like a soccer ball, then a golf ball, a play thing. Then it will look like the world is just a grain of sand. You will be the man, I mean the woman who jumped over the moon. The stars and planets will seem like familiar neighbors. You'll think you hear them laughing, see them winking. You will know for real, the sound of silence. After my first flight, I told myself that all those shapes I saw in the moon were just an illusion, caused by my excitement after being there. I was wondering if I was crazy. Now I know that I should just enjoy whatever I experience. Now I go with the flow and allow myself to be amazed by everything in the universe. I somehow feel like I will never have gone far enough. I will never have dreamt enough or envisioned it all."

The black-curled woman with the dimples just tried to soak in his animated description. It seemed like a fantasy that would be ruined with words. After a few silent minutes she ventured, "Will I get dizzy or anything?"

"No, nothing like that. But when they tell us we can take the harness off, you'll be surprised what the weightlessness feels like. Once we're freed from the harnesses, we'll go for 'a float' together if you want. We can coast by the windows and watch the stars. They'll still look like stars do from earth when the sky is dark. Most of the time though, the sky will be light because we won't be on the 'wrong' side of the earth from the sun." Then Binh paused, "But I'm talking too much. May I ask your name?"

"Of course, my name is Dawn."

"What a perfect name for you."

"Its a family name. My grandmother was Alexis Dawn and my mom was Priscilla Dawn, named after her grandmother. She gave me two middle names after her parents. I'm Dawn Alexis Johanna."

"My name is Binh. I too carry a family name. My grandparents worked in Vietnam during the war. That's where my dad was born. His dad told him he was conceived on a ship going into Vietnam during the war. Binh was the first little boy in Vietnam that my parents fell in love with. They said they always wanted to remember how kind he was to his little sister on those war torn streets so they named their first son Donald Binh. Then he named me the same but I just go by Binh."

"Our grandparents and even parents thought it was science fiction, going to the moon. I'm hoping to see the flag that was placed on the moon by the Apollo 11 astronauts. My grandmother worked for NASA in the 1960s and created the material that was used to make the flag and the astronauts' suits. She retired from Nasa to live in Germany for awhile where her mom lived, when her mom was dying of Alzheimer's. She and my grandpa did a lot of freight ship travel after that. He had been a seaman and they both loved the sea so much."

"A lot of things were science fiction at the turn of the century, that we take for granted now." Like Alzheimer's Disease, there was no cure and no prevention. And animal cruelty. No one could figure out how to prevent overpopulation and the dog-on-the-street problem. Sometimes I feel nostalgic about those times though. Things were slower at the turn of the century. In the early 2000s you could have time for each other. My grandpa always had time for me. It seems like Grandpa is the greatest man in the whole world. Sometimes he can't remember words at all. But He can always smile at me and take my hand. He's had a stroke but I think he's having a good old age, despite his stroke, at least as long as he has Grandma Liesl."

Dawn watched Binh's big brown eyes become completely absorbed in his memories, oblivious to the fact that they were getting ready for a trip to the moon. How much he must love his grandfather. What a wonderful quality that is in a man, the ability to love someone for who they are, with no thought of what that someone can do for you. Dawn felt so drawn to Binh. Could this be what "love at first sight" is like? Her "affection," or "passion," was it? was coming upon her unwanted, unplanned. *No, don't let yourself go there right now,* she said to herself. *Girl, you're just excited about this whole situation right now.* But she couldn't help notice how his brown shirt matched his brown eyes so perfectly and how his smile was welcoming, inviting.

The hostess came around the craft to check the seating and give everyone the first time warning. "Harnesses will be required in about half an hour. If anyone needs to get up, do it now. You will not be allowed out of your seats for one hour after lift off."

"Binh, can I ask you a big favor? When we're ready to lift off, would you mind holding my hand? I won't be so scared if you do."

"It will be a pleasure," Binh grinned. He flipped his head, his wavy auburn hair messed up, and Dawn thought, he looked like a little boy in trouble.

"I think that the original world, millions of years ago must have been governed by centripetal force, that kept animals on the earth and whales in the ocean. Then creatures overcame that force enough to surface or to stand upright. Then they were able to lift off of the earth like birds, in planes. Now look at us. We're governed more by centrifugal force. We can't be kept down. Ever onward, upward, heavenward. I think that God doesn't want to take the credit for the world. He wants us to take the responsibility and be rewarded by what we achieve. We can live at peace with animals and each other if we don't see them all as taking up our space. Our space is endless now. God's force is drawing us outward."   Dawn knew she was being more philosophical and artistic than scientific but felt easy expressing her version of life to Binh. "Did you know that Apollo was named for the Greek god of light, healing, music, poetry, prophesy and beauty?"

Binh added, "Maybe someday we'll even eliminate wars. Only with world peace can we launch a new civilization. I wonder what generation will see that need for peace and finally leap through the frontiers of our waiting, welcoming universe. You know, Apollo wasn't just for America. In 1967 a document was signed by eighty-two countries proclaiming lunar territory international. And the plaque posted with the American flag read 'from planet earth, man first set foot on the moon. We came in peace for all mankind.'

"Dawn, I'm a veterinarian. What kind of work do you do?"

"I teach, but some days I want to be a theologian or a philosopher, some days a gardener. Now as of today..." the wife of a vet was too bold to say right now.

"Yes, as of today what do you want to be?" Binh asked, curiously.

"Oh nothing, maybe an astronomer."

The hostess came by again. "Everybody ready to buckle up?" She looked around, giving time for a last hesitancy, then pronounced, "Its time."

Binh leaned over and helped Dawn with her ankle straps. She rested her head against the head brace and put the strap over her forehead. Her heart was pounding. Which was more enthralling, she pondered, her first trip to the moon, or the firm, gentle, chivalrous touch of Binh Renick?

Now Binh attached his own ankle straps and harness. He turned his head a little toward Dawn before placing his forehead strap so that he could watch her reaction to lift off. Which was more beautiful, he wondered, the shape of the American continent in a blue ocean

- as they rose above it, or those big blue eyes, dimpled cheeks and black bonnet of curls? Binh took Dawn's hand as he had promised. The human enterprise was prepared for lift off.

About the Author :

Lorraine Valentin Sharpe originally from Chicago, IL,

lives in Casselberry, FL

where she retired after fifty years of nursing

and several years a chaplain

in various American and foreign settings.